D0957550

DOUBLE JEOPARDY

You are so there.

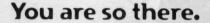

T*WITCHES

1 THE POWER OF TWO
2 BUILDING A MYSTERY
3 SEEING IS DECEIVING
4 DEAD WRONG
5 DON'T THINK TWICE
6 DOUBLE JEOPARDY

T✹WITCHES

H.B. GILMOUR
& RANDI REISFELD

SCHOLASTIC INC.

NEW YORK   TORONTO   LONDON   AUCKLAND   SYDNEY
MEXICO CITY   NEW DELHI   HONG KONG   BUENOS AIRES

ISBN 0-439-24075-1

12 11 10 9 8 7 6 5 4 3 2 1   2 3 4 5 6 7/0

PRINTED IN THE U.S.A.   40
FIRST SCHOLASTIC PRINTING, SEPTEMBER 2002

CHAPTER ONE
FAMILY STRIFE

The front door slammed. Then, again. Just in case the first time wasn't enough to express the fury of the people who came barreling through it.

"I've never been so humiliated!" a woman's shrill voice raged.

"I don't see what the big deal is," came the sulky, defensive response of a teenage boy.

"You don't see what the big deal is?" A man's voice echoed in frustration, "Well, it looks like we're going to have to show you!"

Camryn Barnes heard all this from her second floor bedroom, where she'd been bent over her tenth grade history book, trying — and failing — to concentrate. Even before the sudden loud interruption from downstairs, she'd been antsy and anxious.

Her identical twin, Alexandra Fielding, was pacing all around their shared bedroom, equally flipped out. Too jumpy even to pretend to be dealing with homework, Alex alternated between trading IMs with her Montana homeys, channel surfing, and tuning her guitar.

It was as if someone had told them not to think about a big test that was coming up, and now it was all they could think of. Only, in this case, the test was their long-lost mother.

It was late Friday afternoon and, though neither twin wanted to talk, let alone think about it, both were waiting for a message from her. It might arrive by phone, by e-mail, or possibly drift into their daydreams. Weeks had gone by since they'd been promised it would come. And each passing day made them ever more edgy, made their expected message seem ever more momentous.

So when the door slammed downstairs, it was a relief to be startled out of their shared obsession. Cam threw down her textbook; Alex laid aside the guitar. They bounded down the carpeted steps to the family room, where the weird row raged, out of character and out of control.

David and Emily Barnes, Cam's adoptive parents, were going at it with their son, Dylan. At fourteen, he was a year younger than Cam and Alex, a head taller, and, lately, a whole lot more trouble-prone.

"What's gotten into you?" Emily shrieked at her son, whose blond hair peeked out from under an American flag do-rag.

She took a step toward him and shook her finger. "If you're smoking again or fooling with drugs . . ."

Dylan rolled his cornflower-blue eyes, which matched Emily's own. "Oh, man! Would that make you happy? Would that explain it all?"

Alex's stomach churned. This was a bad one.

Dave's thick mustache, usually turned up with his smile, was drooping with disappointment. His generally jovial manner had done a 180. "Don't you talk to your mother like that. Explain yourself. Now."

Dylan dropped onto the couch. "What's the big deal? I was walking down the street. I wasn't bothering anyone."

"The police picked you up for just walking?" Emily sarcastically interrupted him. "You call kicking over trash cans, dumping garbage all over the street, not bothering anyone?"

Mindlessly tugging at the tiny gold earring he wore, Dylan grumbled defiantly, "I was trying to figure something out. I got frustrated."

"At two in the afternoon, during school hours?" Lawyer Dave objected. "You were cutting."

"Sue me," Dylan mumbled.

Cam flinched. Was he deliberately trying to bait their dad? "What's going on?" she asked nervously.

Alex bounded over to Dylan and touched his arm. "You okay?" she whispered.

Emily growled at them through clenched teeth. "This is between your brother and us. Please leave the room. Both of you."

Two startled pairs of identical silver-gray eyes stared at her. "But Mom . . ." Cam started. She backed off when Dave waved her away.

"Can I just —" Alex asked.

"No, you cannot," Dave snapped. "Go upstairs. Now."

They retreated only as far as the kitchen. Something told them to stick around, not only to eavesdrop, but to prevent Dylan from doing anything he'd regret — which, in his hyper-defiant, self-destructive state, was a given.

As the argument continued to rage in the next room, the twins tried to figure it out. Their brother had been logging more extreme disobedience than extreme sports time lately. He'd already been caught and chewed out for breaking curfew and cutting last-period phys. ed. Worst of all, his grades were in free fall.

Dave and Emily had been all over him, done the "concerned parent, let's communicate" thing. Only now the Marble Bay police were apparently involved. Buh-*bye,* reasonable 'rents — hello, screaming accusations. The home game of family strife was in the penalty phase.

Emily went into default blame. "It's that computer. You're on it morning and night — wasting hours on the Internet or in those chat rooms, instead of doing your homework," she accused.

"I'm not *wasting* hours," Dylan was protesting. "You guys always think the worst. It would never occur to you that I was doing something important, would it? No, to you I'm just the brother of Cam-the-golden-girl and poor-little-orphan-Alex. I'm just some snowboarding slacker with nothing better to do than goof around on the Net."

The tone of Dylan's voice had changed. Belligerent had become bitter. Cam and Alex went into high alert: Something was about to blow.

It was more than a hunch. The gifted twins' talents went way beyond educated guesses and honed instincts. At fifteen, Cam and Alex were capable of knowing and doing things ordinary adults couldn't fathom — including reading each other's minds.

Alex could hear things she shouldn't have been able to — and often didn't want to — like other people's thoughts. Even from the next room, she read Dylan's mind loud and clear.

Cam, who could see and sense things she shouldn't have been able to, like the future — immediate or long-range — "saw" her brother eyeing . . .

Emily's proud new purchase, a pricey "signed McCoy" antique vase!

Alex thought, *He's ballistic, he's actually going to —*

smash it to smithereens!, Cam telepathically finished Alex's panicked thought.

On damage-control patrol, the twins raced into the den in time to see Dylan grab the antique mustard-colored monstrosity.

Can you stop him? Cam anxiously asked her twin.

Too late, Alex responded, as Dylan, fueled by fury, had already drawn his arm back, about to pitch the antique.

Horrified, Emily screamed, "Don't!"

Dave made for his son.

Neither was fast enough to stop Dylan.

Alex was.

Using her powers — the ability to move things just by thinking about them — she closed her eyes and pictured the vase, now arcing through the air, changing direction. It was only inches from the wall, where it would

6 ————————————————————

have been destroyed, when it miraculously made a hairpin turn, and spun toward Cam. With the reflexes of an athlete, she caught it.

It had all happened in a nanosecond, too fast for Emily or Dave to comprehend that something very strange had just happened.

Dylan had no clue he'd just dodged a bullet. Disgusted with himself, he stomped toward the staircase.

CHAPTER TWO
THREE'S A CROWD

Cam hung downstairs with Emily and Dave. Partly to comfort her parents and partly to be sure they were still too unhinged to suspect she and Alex had magically prevented the vase from breaking.

Alex hit the stairs, hurrying after Dylan. They weren't biologically related but the brazen blond boy was the brother she'd have picked if she'd had a choice. Dyl had been reared with Cam, yet he was much more like her, Alex thought.

She shared with Cam's blond bro a love of music, a not-quite mastery of the guitar, and a tendency to find trouble wherever it hid. Not that Dyl qualified as a true delinquent. Proof: Only the sneaky survived; Dylan always got caught.

Alex clumped up the stairs in her scuffed Doc Martens and tapped on Dylan's door. Music, or some ear-shattering attempt at it, had deafened him to her knock. She pounded on his door again and let herself in.

As usual, Dyl's room looked like a cross between a locker room and a laundry hamper. One of his two snowboards was lying across a hill of clothing tossed onto his bed. On his nightstand were the can and cloth he'd been using to wax the board. His guitar, plugged into an amp hidden under another mound of clothes, leaned against his dresser with, Alex was pleased to note, a couple of pages of lyrics she'd written during one of their sessions. In the middle of it all, his back to the door, clicking away at the forbidden computer, was the bad boy himself.

Sidestepping the floor mess, Alex pushed the OFF button on his CD player. "'S'up?" she said, coming up behind him. "You okay?"

Dylan jumped. "Yeah, yeah," he answered, spinning around on his computer chair. "Cool. Gnarly. Okay? I . . . I just need to be alone —"

"What're you doing?" She peered at the screen and saw that he was having a chat-room convo with someone named KC. "Besides what you're not supposed to?"

"What're you, on their side now?" Dyl grumbled.

"Yeah, right." Alex dismissed the lame remark. "Who's KC? And why is he important enough to get you in more trouble than you're already in?"

Dylan's face turned to stone. "Why are you looking over my shoulder? Who I'm writing to is none of your . . ." He stopped, suddenly realizing Alex had only come to help. "Look," he said, his eyes pleading with her, "it's important — and private. Do me a solid and just go now, okay?"

Alex shrugged. "If that's what you want. But if you change your mind . . . if you need me . . ."

"I know," he answered.

Alex took the shortcut to the room she shared with Cam, through the bathroom that connected their den with Dylan's. What she ran into puzzled her. Cam was at the sink, putting on makeup.

"Uh . . . what are you doing? Going somewhere?" Alex asked.

"Taking advantage of the cease-fire," Cam answered as she applied a final touch of lip gloss. "Going out for pizza. So are you. C'mon, get ready. Beth got her permit. We're all going out to celebrate."

Alex was truly bewildered. "Was there a memo I didn't get? I thought we agreed to wait until —"

"Until what?" Cam said, sighing. She turned away from the mirror to stare at her sister. Which, it occurred to Alex, was totally redundant, since they looked exactly alike.

Except for their hair — Cam's gleaming auburn, the result of her ritual twenty minutes of daily shampoo-conditioner-blow-drying vs. Alex's two seconds of head shaking and hand-raking her choppy, bleached 'do.

And their attitudes — they didn't always think alike. And right now, the difference was total.

Alex followed Cam back into their bedroom, where her twin began the process of figuring out what to wear. She decided on a baby-blue sweater set and black boot-cut jeans and began to pull the combination out of the closet.

Alex, in an old sweatshirt and faded jeans, plopped down on her bed, hands clasped behind her head, staring out at an ice-white moon. "She said she'd call."

"She *said* she'd be in touch," Cam corrected.

"Yeah. Soon."

"It's been a month, Als." Cam wriggled into the jeans. "We've been waiting for her for a month. Make that a year. Whoops, try all our lives. She can wait for us tonight."

"Wow, cruel and unusual comeback, Cami." Alex tried to make a joke of it. It didn't work.

It was just too big.

It was all about the twins' birth mother. Miranda. A woman they'd never met but had wondered about, obsessed over, probably every day for nearly a year. She'd been assumed dead, until the twins themselves made the startling discovery that she was alive.

Miranda. She'd called them just last month. Her voice on the telephone had been soft, sweet, eager.

Nervous, Cam had thought, uncertain.

Quivering with excitement, Alex was convinced, with joy!

She'd promised to visit them soon.

So far, "soon" had totaled a month — which was, not so weirdly, about as long as their nerves had been jangling.

Tonight's family feud had shaken up Cam. She was out of patience. Much as she loved Dylan, she didn't understand why he was purposefully upsetting their parents. Especially Emily — in most ways, her real mom. There was way too much going on at home, Cam decided. The Miranda issue would have to be shelved. For now. She guessed.

Alex wasn't as attached to Emily, hadn't grown up with her. Alex's "mom-eries" were all about Sara Fielding — in every way, *her* real mom.

As for Miranda, Alex was perplexed about what was taking so long. Four weeks, going on five. She had to admit — to herself only — that while she longed for the day they'd meet, she was worried about it, too.

What if Miranda didn't like them? Didn't like *her*. Unlike Cam, she wasn't everybody's cup of chai. And she didn't have a substitute family to fall back on.

Both of Alex's adoptive parents, Ike and Sara, were dead. At least Cam still had Dave and Emily, who'd adopted her as an infant, and Dylan, their bio-child.

Different as they were about some things, Alex thought, watching her sister's endless prep for a date with a pizza, she and Cam shared more than being adopted.

Neither of them had known she was, or had, a twin until a year ago when, at age fourteen, they'd met by accident.

And, although both of them had always wondered why they weren't exactly like other kids, they hadn't realized they were witches.

Now they were fifteen. Cam's 'rents had become Alex's court-authorized legal guardians. And of all the uncertainties in their still-strange lives, they were sure of this: They were teens. Twins. Witches.

T'Witches.

"Look," Cam said, reading Alex's mind, "I'm just as anxious and scared about meeting her as you are. I mean, I'm dying to. But —"

"Dying? Interesting choice of words, Camryn," Alex

pointed out, turning away from her sister and back to the comforting moonlight.

Cam knew what her twin meant. Alex was convinced that their uncle, the billionaire warlock, Lord Thantos, had been involved in the long-ago disappearance — and now sudden and strange reappearance — of their mother.

Thantos, the brutal and powerful warlock, had supposedly murdered his own brother, their dad, Aron, on the very day of their birth on Coventry Island, home to a community of witches and warlocks. He'd been on their trail ever since.

If Alex was right, if evil Uncle T was behind their mother's recent, startling phone call to them, then *dying* was not just an apt word but a good possibility.

A weird smell hit Alex's nostrils. "What's that new cologne called?" she asked, wrinkling her nose. "Displeasure?"

Cam looked like she'd caught the same scent. Her face went all sweaty. She sat down suddenly at the edge of Alex's bed and threw off her cardigan. "It's warm in here."

"And getting hotter," a deep voice rumbled.

Alex and Cam spun toward the sound.

And gasped.

Leaning back in Cam's chair, his hobnail boots resting on her desk, his broad, black-cloaked back to them, was Thantos.

14 ———————————————————

CHAPTER THREE
THE VISITOR

They'd run into him at an old abandoned gas station out in the woods. They'd felt him watching them at a theme park in Montana. He'd tried to snare them at a dismal rave in a tawdry warehouse district.

But this was worse. Much worse.

Their murderous uncle had trespassed on the one place they'd thought was sacred and safe. Thantos had shattered the sanctity of their home.

Alex and Cam seized each other's hands. Their touch acted like a conduit. Fear pulsed wildly between them.

"I know you're in a hurry." Slowly, casually, the massive warlock spun to face them. "I won't keep you long," he said, letting his feet fall with a bang that should have alerted Dave and Emily downstairs. But didn't.

Cam began to feel light-headed, but a reckless rush of adrenaline surged through Alex.

"What are you doing here?!" she demanded, forgetting who she was shouting at — namely, one of the world's most powerful . . .

And dangerous, Cam silently reminded her sister.

. . . Warlocks. Lord Thantos, their uncle, was a third-degree tracker whose status and skill was equal only to that of their old friend Karsh — in Karsh's long-past heyday.

Age was not the only difference between the two men. Karsh, wizened and white-haired, had cared for and protected the twins their entire lives. He'd chosen parents to adopt them and appointed Ileana, a headstrong but fiercely dedicated young witch, to be their guardian. While Thantos had tried only to lure and trap them.

Their uncle was studying them now, his black-bearded face frowning.

Despite her outburst, Alex was shaking. Remembering the dizziness his glare could cause, Cam had lowered her eyes. She would not look directly at him.

He shook his head. "Amazing," he muttered, then sighed, sounding almost melancholy. "Do you have any idea how much you resemble your father?"

16

The father you murdered? Cam thought but dared not say.

Of course, Thantos heard her anyway.

"I see you're not up on the news," he roared, cured of his sentimental moment. "I've been exonerated. Cleared of all charges." He stood and began to stomp back and forth before them. "Oh, dear," he said sarcastically in a wheedling voice, "have Karsh and Ileana kept you in the dark? Failed to fill you in on the happenings that made history on Coventry Island last week? Check with your guardians. I had nothing to do with Aron's death. I did, however, have much to do with your mother's survival —"

"We know where she is," Alex blurted.

"You had her locked away in an institution," Cam accused.

For a time they had believed Miranda was dead. Once they suspected she was alive, they began to search for her. Recently, a truly bizarre set of circumstances had proved that their mother was living hidden away in an institution — the exact same exclusive clinic to which Cam's friend Brianna had been sent.

Bree's e-mails about a fellow patient who was looking after her — a beautiful woman who wore her long auburn hair in a single braid, had eyes the same silvergray color as the twins', and wore a necklace similar to the precious ones Cam and Alex's birth father had made for them — led to a phone call from the birth mother they'd never met. It was during that brief call that Miranda had promised to visit them soon.

Thantos stopped pacing and whirled on them. "I did what was best for your mother."

"You locked her away," Cam persisted.

"But we found her," Alex boasted.

"Not without my help." Now it was Thantos's turn to gloat. "Who do you think chose the clinic your friend was in — the place where young Brianna just happened to meet a lovely, lonely woman with a necklace much like your own?"

Shocked, Cam and Alex looked at each other. "No," Cam declared.

"Don't believe him," Alex advised. "You couldn't have arranged that. You're not that powerful," she challenged her uncle.

He was angry, weary, frustrated. "Foolish fledglings!" With a wave of his hand, his nieces flew backward, landing against Cam's bed. "Sit down!" Thantos ordered.

Eyes wide, hearts racing again, they did.

From beneath his velvet cape, the hulking tracker drew a leather pouch and took a number of objects from it. Among them, Cam saw the translucent pink glow of rose quartz. And Alex smelled mint and the subtle balm of chamomile.

"Is that all Ileana and old Karsh have taught you?" Thantos asked disdainfully. He opened his huge hand. "What of moonstone, agate geode, or iron pyrite? And this root, have you learned what mandrake is for? Or how to release the power of valerian?"

On Cam's dresser sat one of the scented candles her friend Amanda had given her. "Light it!" their uncle ordered. Cam's eyes flew open and focused on the candle. A familiar heat rose inside her, nipped at her eyes, first sharpening her sight and then, as the candlewick blazed, blurring it with tears.

Alex watched, fascinated, hypnotized, as the warlock tossed bits of mandrake root and valerian into the flame.

"What do you see?" he asked in a voice soft and dark as his black velvet cape.

In the dancing firelight, they saw — Cam, who was used to visions, and Alex, who had never experienced one — they saw *Dylan*!

Helpless. Terrified. Trapped.

He was inside a dark iron box, stumbling amid empty cartons, bubble wrap, and packing crates, a trash-smeared container smaller than a room, larger than a coffin. Dylan was trying to scale its rubbish-greased sides when a roar caught his attention — and theirs. As he looked up, Cam and Alex could see through his eyes a mechanical mouth opening, its jaws lined with steel teeth.

The roar grew in intensity until Alex had to clamp her hands over her aching ears. And as the clanking howl increased, the steel mouth widened and lowered as if it would crush the entire iron box in which Dylan was caught.

He was inside a Dumpster, Cam realized. The noise was the ruckus of a big garbage truck backing up . . . about to seize the trash, and Dylan, from the Dumpster . . . into its iron-clawed maw.

"No!" Cam shouted. "Stop!"

With the hiss of a giant snake, the candle flame went out.

Thantos smiled at them. "It was only a thought."

Cam had experienced such "thoughts" before, only she knew them as premonitions, visions of what was to come.

"No," Alex whispered to her. "Don't worry. Dylan's not trapped in that disgusting contraption. He's safe. He's in his room. I saw him a minute ago."

"She's right," their uncle said. "It was a mere exercise . . . a demonstration. But accidents do happen —"

"Why are you here?" Alex asked. "What do you want?"

"Only to help you," Thantos answered, sounding improbably gentle and sincere. "To help you and Miranda. I know how eager you are to meet her at last, to look upon your true mother and see a part of yourselves. I know you have been waiting for her to call you again. But she can't. She won't. She will not call or come to you unless I bring her."

"When?" Cam asked.

"It's been fifteen years," Alex murmured. "How much longer are you going to keep her locked away, hidden —"

"You mean," Thantos said, "how much longer will you have to wait? Not long." He smiled. "A bit longer than your friends at the pizza shop have been waiting for you —"

"Whoops," Cam yipped, as if waking from a dream. "We're supposed to be at PITS —"

Alex glared at her. "How can you think about that at a time like this? Don't you want to see her?"

"Of course," Cam told her sister. "More than anything."

They heard Thantos chuckle and turned toward him. Where the hulking tracker had stood, now only a coil of dark smoke drifted, and a distant, retreating voice announced: "As my mother, your grandmother Leila, used to say, 'Be careful what you wish for.'"

CHAPTER FOUR
WHO ARE YOU?

Be careful what you wish for . . .

Ileana sat on the cool sand, facing the ocean. Her tangled hair and solemn face were damp with sea spray carried on the evening breeze. Her eyes were sad, unfocused. But Leila's words sang in her head like vengeful children, taunting her.

Nah-nah-nah-nah-nah! Be careful what you wish for!

Ileana had gotten everything she'd wished for. Always.

It had been a hallmark of her personality. Willful, bossy, beautiful, and bright, the vain young witch had never been one to wait her turn.

She had prided herself on making things happen.

She had wished for Truth and Justice. And she had made *this* happen — this lonely, gloomy exile.

The joke was on her.

Truth: A long-standing wrong had been righted.

A murderer had been exposed and punished.

The dark cloud of doubt that had hung over Coventry Island for fifteen years had finally been lifted.

Single-handedly, Ileana had done what no one else had been able to do.

Only somewhere on the road to Justice, Ileana had been robbed.

Some would call it comeuppance.

The haughty me-first witch with the superiority complex had been kicked off her high horse. Tumbled. Humbled. No one would recognize her now — neither her fervent enemies nor those who professed to love her.

Here in this tropical paradise, Ileana was ghostly pale from days spent in a darkened bungalow. Her normally vibrant gray eyes were clouded, her lustrous pale hair tangled and matted.

What did it matter that others would not know her? She didn't recognize herself.

Amnesia? If only she had it. Alone on the beach, Ileana shook her head.

Her problem was that she *could* remember. All of it.

As Leila had prophesied, what she had wished for — and passionately believed in — had turned on her viciously. Betrayed her, like so many of those she'd trusted.

She had believed herself to be an orphan, lucky enough to have been reared by Lord Karsh, the good and powerful old warlock who'd taught her everything she knew about the craft, about life. Except the one thing she'd wished for — the name of her father.

Now she knew it.

She'd wished for a soul mate and believed she'd found one in Brice Stanley, a world-renowned movie star and secret warlock who, Ileana had been confident, loved her.

But Brice had testified on behalf of Thantos DuBaer — Ileana's sworn enemy.

What she believed, with every bone and breath in her body, was that Thantos DuBaer was a murderer, the vicious killer who had slaughtered the twins' father — and possibly their mother — and had been trying for years to snare her young charges, Camryn and Alexandra.

So passionately had Ileana wished to expose Thantos, to bring him to justice, that she had done the nearly impossible.

She had summoned the restless spirit of Leila, the deceased matriarch of the DuBaer clan, mother of

Thantos, his miserable sibling Fredo, and their murdered brother, Aron.

Surely their mother knew the truth.

Ileana had wished for Leila to settle the matter of who had killed gentle Lord Aron. Again, her wish had come true.

Leila had identified Fredo as the fiend, proving Ileana wrong and turning the monstrous Lord Thantos into a slandered hero.

And Fredo, spiteful, cruel, inept, with no sense of right and wrong, had shouted out the final truth. That Thantos, the warlock Ileana had despised all her life and had tried desperately to bring down, was her father.

The lazy waves now washed over the dejected young witch's sandaled feet. She should get up, Ileana realized. The evening was turning cold. The tide was coming in. She should get up. But why, for what?

As if in answer, raucous laughter drifted to her from down the beach. If there was anything she didn't want to hear right now it was laughter and young voices, loud, elated, and carefree.

Ileana dragged herself to her feet. Standing on the same lonely strip of beach she'd paced for the past several nights, she gazed out at the ocean. As foamy water lapped the hem of her turquoise caftan, she noticed a piece of driftwood bobbing on the water. It was directionless, unanchored, tossed this way and that at nature's whim.

A perfect metaphor, Ileana thought. In it, she recognized her new self.

The partying grew louder, wilder. She would have liked to ignore it, but she couldn't. Along with the wind-carried noise came a feeling of looming danger. The awareness broke through her self-absorbed funk, and she tried to zoom-lens in on the bash down the beach.

Had she gotten sand in her eyes? Had staring out at the ocean dulled her sight? She saw a shaft of leaping orange light but couldn't make out exactly what it was.

For a moment, she thought: So what? Who cares?

Her sense of jeopardy, of children in trouble, grew. Despite her cynicism, Ileana found herself drawn to the unknown trouble. She tried to lift off, to levitate, and catch an airstream that would transport her to the mishap at once. Instead, her wet feet churned clumsily through the sand.

What she finally saw was a group of teenagers, some lounging on blankets, others kicking up sand, chasing one another around the flaring light of a large campfire.

A campfire, Ileana noticed from some yards away, that was being fed and spread by the wind. Hissing red embers shot into the air, landing on blankets that were much too close to the fire. Some of the laughing children stamped on the hot coals with their bare feet, smothering wayward flames.

But two youngsters sat on an old bedspread with their backs to the light, unaware that the flames had begun to lick the dry chenille edges of their blanket.

Ileana called out to the couple and, when they didn't hear her, she sent them a psychic 911, ordering them to get up, get off and away from the blanket. But they seemed not to have gotten the message.

Finally, when she was within earshot of them, Ileana cupped her hands around her mouth and shouted, "Fire!"

The moment the shocked duo heard her, they rose and ran. Ileana focused on the now-flaming blanket. Telekinesis, the ability to move things through mental concentration — one of Alex's precocious gifts — was old magick to Ileana. She pictured the flaming bedspread lifting off the sand, drifting up, and plunging into the ocean.

She was about to turn aside and go on her self-satisfied way when she realized with horror that the blanket hadn't moved.

But the fire had. Hot embers were spattering the clothing of several children. There was smoke coming off the rolled-up cuff of one boy's khaki pants; soon his trousers would be aflame. And the flames would spread. Six teenagers, the same age as Cam and Alex, Ileana realized, might be burned.

Quickly, she began to perform a spell. The words sounded hollow to her. The crystal in her hand remained lifelessly cold, the herbs in her pouch dry as dust. Suddenly, Ileana had an idea of what was happening and gasped in terror.

In a flash, she remembered when she was a child, about the age of these rash teens, only a year younger than Camryn and Alexandra were now.

She remembered how Miranda, their mother, had lost her husband and been consumed by a grief so terrible that it had muted her magical powers.

Was that what was happening to Ileana? Were all the awful truths she'd learned too fast breaking her spirit and stealing her skills?

Panicked screams pierced the night as the fire continued its deadly, scorching spread. A girl swatted at her sarong, trying to beat out the flames. But it wasn't enough.

Ileana tried again. Telekinesis, spells, psychic messages, levitation. Nothing. She was helpless in the face of real danger. She could not do the most important thing she was sworn to do as a witch. She could not help.

The young girl was screaming.

"Get down!" Ileana shouted at her. "Roll in the sand. Wade into the surf. Hurry!"

She could not count on her voice rising above the noise of the ocean and the panicked shouts, so she ran from one child to another, pulling them down, pushing them toward the water.

While they shrieked and rolled and splashed and turned a disaster into an adventure, Ileana stood, stunned, staring at the campfire.

Her powers, her gifts, all that made her an enviable witch had been swept away.

CHAPTER FIVE
A PREMONITION

Spindly and tall, his muscles taut, Karsh clasped both hands tightly around the broom handle. He swung it like a golf pro, confident, steady, accurate. *Swoosh!* Cobwebs disintegrated. Dust balls scattered like mice fleeing a cat. And wasn't he, he thought happily as he took another swipe across the wooden floor, quite the cat. What did the kids say? The hep cat, the cool cat? What might young Camryn and Alex say? Something like that. He grinned.

The recent trial, at which he'd represented the people of Coventry Island, had rejuvenated him. For the first time in a long time, Karsh felt truly invigorated, back to health, in top form. He scanned the sitting room of his cozy Coventry Island cottage, anxious to give it a thorough cleaning. He flexed a bicep. Like the broom he gripped securely, there was nothing he couldn't handle.

Unexpectedly, Karsh caught a glimpse of himself in the now-gleaming polished wood floor. He laughed. His reflection mocked his feelings of vitality. He looked like a wrinkled old man, with nappy white hair, skin so crinkly and papery thin as to nearly be translucent, ancient eyes hooded and dimmed by age. Well, what was that other expression? Can't judge a book by its cover?

His blue eyes danced as he crossed the room to his wall of bookcases, crammed with dozens of volumes. The cracked spines had names such as *The Universal Craft Guide, Herbs of Coventry Island, Forgiveness or Vengeance: Righting Ancient Wrongs, Spells to Conjure With.* . . .

The handsome leather-bound books might deceive the unschooled, but any wise witch would realize the pages held incantations, tenets of herbal science, laws of tracking, of transmutating — all practices of the craft. Some books had been hollowed out so sacred amulets could be stored safely inside them.

For instance, the one titled *Sticks and Stones* was really a velvet-lined box filled with unpolished gems, mineral-laden amulets, and ancient crystals. Few would know that among the geological trinkets were five sacred stones, gathered from five hallowed sites: ancient Egypt, Mesopotamia, Machu Picchu, the caves of Coventry Island, and Salem, Massachusetts.

There were other kinds of volumes as well, books that told of ancient curses, of how to do harm. Karsh had often thought of disposing of those permanently. But he could not. Yet.

There were photos interspersed with the books. Snapshots of his family, now all long gone, and portraits of friends — mostly of the fledglings he'd taught through the years. He picked up one of Ileana, his most volatile charge, and shook his head sadly. What she must be going through now!

He gently removed the photo from its glassed-in frame. Hidden behind it was a picture Karsh could neither bring himself to toss out nor look at. He picked it up and stared at it. Taken long ago, it was a snapshot of a young warlock standing tall, smiling broadly, his chest puffed out. The young Karsh's arm was casually flung around the shoulder of another man, this one also young, a bit shorter and broader, and also grinning.

Nathaniel DuBaer. His long-dead best friend. They'd been so full of hope in those days, firmly believing that the best of life was there for the taking. That they were invincible. But fate had other plans.

Glass shattered, splintering all over his freshly

swept floor. Karsh would realize later that the framed photograph had slipped out of his hands and crashed to the floor. As he'd been staring at it, a familiar sensation swept over him. No matter how many times it happened, he still feared it: the icy chill that swirled about him, the constriction of his throat, the beads of sweat forming on his forehead. As always, Karsh's ears rang loudly, obliterating any other sound. His eyes stung, his vision blurred, then sharpened.

And Karsh saw:

A forest, deep with trees, yet swampy, indicating water nearby — a pond, a lake, a bay, perhaps. Yes. A handsome cove, edged in tall reeds and cattails and a narrow, rocky beach. But in the woods, through an aisle of towering evergreens, a mystic circle walled with rocks made his blood run cold. In horror, he watched, repulsed yet hypnotized, as a gaunt form in a funereal cape turned to him, eyes wide with shock. Gasping, grabbing his temples, the stunned figure staggered backward, then crumpled in the dirt.

Karsh's own hands flew to his head to stop the spreading and deepening pain. He heard screams again, far away but familiar. And then everything faded.

The unnerved warlock gripped the bookcase to steady himself and took a tentative step forward. Shards of glass crunched under his slippers. His head pounded.

Visions such as these, as he'd taught Camryn, signaled a premonition, a psychic preview of an event that would occur at a later time. Sometimes it felt frightening and dangerous, predicting something bad; often it was hard to figure out exactly what it meant.

But Karsh knew precisely what this vision had forecast. Angrily, he slammed his fist on the bookcase. He had much to do now, and he had to act quickly.

Leaving the broken glass where it lay, he yanked the *Sticks and Stones* book from its perch and flung it open. Eyes closed, he sifted through the stones, recognizing the ones he sought by touch.

The sacred five would tell him what he needed to know immediately — where Ileana was. She'd fled Coventry Island, wanting time and space to cope with the trial's revelations. And Karsh had promised not to seek her out.

His premonition forced him to break that promise.

He cleared the top of his ancient desk and placed four of the stones in an exact pattern, laying the tiger-eye in the center. He lit a candle and, with intensity, performed the Calling.

Light radiated from deep within each stone. Each beam strengthened the glowing color of the next. Together they formed a powerful rainbow. If the ritual were done correctly, with a pure heart, he would find her in the tigereye. Be able to summon her in a flash, when and if he had to.

Karsh stared into the golden gleam of the center stone — and saw Ileana.

She was alone on a beach, staring out at the sea. Instantly, he knew where his dejected charge had gone. He exhaled fully and allowed relief to sweep through him.

Which might have been why he didn't hear them, or pick up the scent of cheap cologne and oily hair tonic, and didn't intuit the danger; maybe that was why he found himself ambushed.

Two intruders violently kicked in his front door and came at him with fists raised.

He knew his attackers. Tsuris and Vey, the vicious sons of Fredo DuBaer, had recently arrived on the island to attend their father's trial. Now, fueled by misguided allegiance to the parent they rarely saw, the mindless bullies wanted revenge.

"Where is she, old man?" Tsuris, the taller of the deluded duo, demanded as he took a menacing step toward Karsh.

"Where is Ileana, the traitor who put our father in jail? She's not at home," snarled the clumpy, red-faced Vey. "We already searched her place. You know where she is. Give it up!"

Karsh tried to reason with them. "Your anger is misdirected. Ileana did nothing more than open the door, allowing the truth to finally come out."

"Truth? You old faker! You can't fool us," Tsuris growled. "It's a scheme to smear our good name, cheat us out of what's owed to us."

So that was it? These insolent fools, raised in California by a greedy mother who'd divorced Fredo years ago, felt threatened. They didn't care about their father, only that their share of the inheritance of DuBaer Industries might be affected.

Karsh shook his head. Selfish and stupid begat selfish and stupid. There was no reasoning with either.

"Tell us where she is right now, or you'll regret it . . . if you live to!" Vey leaned in threateningly.

Ordinarily, Karsh could have dispensed with these roughnecks. With a flick of his hand, he could have turned Vey into the lumpy toad he resembled and Tsuris, whose bleached hair stood on end, into a prickly cactus. But strong and healthy as Karsh had felt moments ago, age had slowed him and the premonition had broken his concentration. Just enough for the dunderheaded duo to act.

With a brutal shove, Tsuris knocked Karsh down. The surprised tracker landed hard on his back on the cold stone floor. Waving the cane the old warlock had used during his illness, Vey ordered him to stay down.

The ruffians raged through the cottage, flinging open doors, wrecking what they could — out of sheer spite — knocking over furniture, tearing down drying herbs, breaking crockery and glassware in their way.

The pain in Karsh's head was intense. Just before everything went black, he heard the sickening clatter of his sacred stones tumbling from the table and skidding across the slate floor.

CHAPTER SIX
A RESTLESS NIGHT

PITS was crowded, noisy, and warm with the scrumptious, oven-fresh scent of pizza. Five of the "Six Pack," Cam's crew, plus Alex, were cozily packed into the big booth up front — where everyone who came or went could pause to chat, wave, or check them out admiringly.

"Let's get out of here," Alex whispered to her sister.

Cam nodded but made no move to leave.

Neither of them was hungry. For the past fifteen minutes, they'd picked at their slices, nodded, and pretended to be part of the Friday evening fun and festivities. But their attention was elsewhere.

Cam couldn't forget the ugly vision Thantos had painted for them or shake the awful feeling that it was a peek into the future, not some random event their uncle had conjured.

Alex was equally preoccupied, but she was thinking of their mother and whether Thantos had told them the truth when he'd said Miranda wouldn't call again or come to see them without his . . . permission.

Cam had been honestly pleased for her tall, curly-haired best friend Beth, who'd just gotten her driver's permit. But after giving Beth a brief "Go, girl," she'd quickly tuned out.

Alex had tried to listen as Kristen Hsu, tossing her cascading, stick-straight, pitch-black hair over her shoulders, delivered the latest word on Bree — who was still dealing with her anorexia at the same California clinic where their mom was supposed to be.

And it took all the energy they had to fake interest in the newest school tragedy being batted around by Sukari and Amanda.

"Someone said it was a skateboarding accident," gullible Amanda was saying. "But then I heard she slipped on the stairs —"

"And landed on her eyeball? I think not," Sukari noted dryly.

"They're investigating her folks," Kristen confidently chimed in. "They always go after the 'rents when child abuse is suspected."

"Kenya is not exactly a child," Beth pointed out. "She's . . . Cami, isn't she in Dylan's class?"

Hearing her brother's name jolted Cam. "What?" she asked, startled.

Something about a girl in his class, Alex silently informed her.

"Kenya Carson," Beth said. "Isn't she in —"

"I'm sorry," Cam said. "I'm just —" She looked at her sister for help.

"She's . . . not feeling well," Alex decided. "I told her we should've stayed home but —"

"Oh, no." Kris shrank away from Cam. "That's all I need. My sister just got over the flu —"

Cam looked around, dazed. She did feel sick. And she probably looked it, too.

"Come on, let's go," Alex urged her.

"I'm sure it's nothing," Cam told her buds, sliding out of the booth. "I probably just need a good night's sleep. But Als is right. We should go home."

"If it were daytime, I could drive you," Beth said.

"Our bikes have lights. And there's a moon out. No probs," Alex assured her.

A good night's sleep was not an option.

Cam wanted to look in on Dylan before they went to their room, but Alex didn't.

"He's cool. I checked him out before we left," Alex said, walking past Dyl's closed door. "Just before Uncle Devious popped up. Do you think he was telling the truth?"

Cam shuddered. "I hope not."

"I wasn't talking about his teen horror flick starring Dylan Barnes." After cautiously opening the door to their room and finding it free of uninvited guests, Alex threw her hooded sweatshirt on her bed. "I meant Miranda. Do you think he's the only one who can get her to come here? Because if that's true, it really reeks. I mean, she's our mom. You'd think she'd want to see us as badly as we want —"

"What was it he said?" Cam asked, pulling the scrunchie off her ponytail and shaking her hair free. "Accidents do happen."

"He was just trying to scare us," Alex decided as Cam headed for the bathroom that linked their room with Dylan's.

"Trying?" Cam exclaimed. "I'd say he was totally successful." She glanced at the door leading to her brother's room — and felt a pull to just peek in. . . .

"Have you ever thought about why he wants us?" Alex called, distracting her.

"Who, Thantos?" Cam's worrywart impulse faded. "Duh! Have you ever thought about coloring your hair?"

By the time she came out in her pj's, Alex — wearing a ripped and threadbare T-shirt that had belonged to her adoptive mom, Sara — was already in bed.

"No, I'm serious, Cami. Let's face it," Alex said as her identical twin climbed into her identical twin bed, "when it comes to the craft, we're good, but we're not that good. If he really wanted to, Big Unc could brutally blow us away. Why hasn't he?"

Cam shrugged, then clicked off the light on the table between them. "Gotta say, I just sort of bought Ileana's explanation —"

Ileana, their high-strung but nevertheless extremely bright guardian, believed that Thantos wanted to "turn" the twins; to bring them, and the remarkable powers they were destined to possess, over to the dark side; to have them serve their uncle's greed for wealth and power rather than the urgent needs of humanity.

Ileana also believed that failing to persuade them to work for him, Thantos would not hesitate to kill them.

For a while, neither of them spoke, but each knew the other was awake and afflicted with "monkey mind" — which, according to Cam's friend Amanda, was a Zen expression for wildly obsessive thinking.

"Okay, a dollar fifty for your thoughts," Alex finally broke the silence. "I mean, I'm kind of focusing on *when,* while you're all about *what,* right?"

"I guess," Cam confessed. "I mean, *when* we'll get to meet our mom isn't really up to us, is it? But I can't help thinking about *what* she's really like."

"And your conclusion?" Alex prodded.

"Gentle," Cam said. "You know, like, calm and kind and loving . . . And probably kind of nervous about meeting us. Like wanting to make a good impression. I mean, she's a mom, right?"

"Dude, she's also a witch," Alex pointed out. "Think about it. She's survived the murder of her husband, the loss of us — no big deal, right? — and fifteen years in captivity, like, practically in prison or whatever. Fifteen years locked away from her Coventry Island friends and family —"

"So what are you saying?" Cam asked defensively. "You think she's going to be like some ex-con?"

"No, but I don't see her as all sweet and soft and momlike," her sister retorted. "I think she's probably incredibly strong. More like some fierce goddess, you know, like this temporarily sidelined superwoman —"

"Alex! She cried on the phone. She cried when she heard our voices," Cam said impatiently. "What are we, Kryptonite?"

"Good night," Alex said.

"Yeah, really," Cam grumbled.

Half an hour later, she added, "They both had gray eyes. Weird, huh?"

"Our parents," Alex responded without skipping a beat. "Bree said Miranda had the same color eyes as ours, but big, bad Thantos claims we resemble our dad —"

"Bree said she was very beautiful," Cam murmured.

"That nails it." Alex laughed. "Obviously, Uncle T was right. We must look like our father."

Cam giggled. Their dad, Aron, they'd discovered, had been the middle child of three — born between tall, hulking Thantos and small, skinny, goat-bearded Fredo. "Ugh," Cam said, "I hope *he* didn't look anything like his brothers."

They were quiet for a time. When Alex next glanced at the digital clock between them, she saw that it was three A.M. "Which brings us back to *when*," she said.

"Huh?" Cam had dozed off.

"Maybe we should play along. Pretend we're, like, totally ready to intern at his company, go with him, — just as soon as he gets us together with Miranda. What do you think?"

Camryn shifted sleepily. "I think we're doing it again," she said, yawning. "Trying to figure out everything on our own when it's clear we should be asking for Karsh's and Ileana's help."

"Cami," Alex confessed, "I've been trying to contact them all night. They're not answering —" A moment later, she sat up abruptly. Hugging herself against a cold breeze that had suddenly raised goose bumps on the nape of her neck, she called softly, "Cam?"

"I . . . I'm here," her sister replied through chattering teeth. "And, er . . . I think he is, too. I just felt his presence."

"Thantos. I know," Alex whispered. "I . . . smelled him."

"And what do I smell like?" The sheer window curtains rose and fluttered, as if driven by their uncle's booming voice. "Snakes and snails and puppy-dog tails?"

"Cloves and wet earth and stinging ice," Alex replied shakily.

"Excellent," Thantos said. "Your senses are remarkably honed. However, I'm not here to judge your skills but rather to demonstrate mine. Go to the sacred tree in Mariner's Park —"

"Our mother?" Alex asked, shivering again.

"When?" Cam demanded.

"Now," their uncle said. "As on the day of your birth, between the rising sun and waning moon, she will welcome you."

CHAPTER SEVEN
A RIDE IN THE PARK

Cam hadn't fallen off a bike since she was six. Now, on this pale moonlit night, just before dawn, she was trembling so hard, she kept losing her balance on the red mountain bike she'd had for years. Her palms were clammy; she was shivering and sweating at the same time. Like a fever.

She'd rushed out of the house so fast, she'd forgotten her wallet and cell phone, hadn't bothered to fix her hair, or even leave a note for her parents. By Cam standards, she was a wreck.

Alex was faring no better. Trying, and failing, to keep a calm exterior, she pedaled next to Cam, as obviously unprepared for chattering teeth, sweaty palms on the handlebars, and difficulty breathing as her twin.

For a while, they were silent, each lost in thought.

Memories — not their own but stories they'd been told by others, by Karsh, by Ileana, Thantos, and even Fredo — came flooding back as every rotation of their bike wheels took them closer.

Cam recalled the first stunning time she and Alex had heard Miranda's voice, a flashback that occurred spontaneously when their sun and moon necklaces fused together for the very first time.

And now they were about to meet her. Nearly one year since they'd met each other.

In that time, Cam had gone through a million imaginary conversations with Miranda. Sometimes the connection was instant and natural. She and Miranda laughed, embraced, caught up on the missing years. It would be like, Cam thought, meeting a friend you hadn't seen in a long time and marveling at how easy it was to pick up the familiar threads of conversation.

She'd even envisioned introducing Miranda to Dave and Emily and Dylan. Somehow, all of them would live as one family, united.

There were other fantasies. In these, Miranda had been aloof, standoffish. She'd never really wanted to be in their lives. In spite of everything Cam and Alex had been led to believe, she had ditched them knowingly and was now forced by Thantos to see them again. After which, she'd hurriedly leave.

Though she would never admit it, Cam almost preferred the "rejection" daydreams. The ones in which she'd meet Miranda only once. Mystery solved. Then she could finally get her life back, the fun one she used to have.

She shuddered suddenly. Mystery. What was the meaning of Thantos's grotesque Dylan-in-the-Dumpster trick? It had been meant to scare them, to prove Thantos's power, nothing more, Cam tried in vain to reassure herself. Her heart thudded and panic struck at the very idea. Plus, she didn't have her cell phone. What if something really did happen to Dyl and he tried desperately to reach her?

Without meaning to, Cam hit the brakes abruptly.

"Watch out!" Alex shouted. "What's wrong with you? You practically crashed into me."

Cam swallowed. "Not even close. And just because you're nervous doesn't give you the right to be such an irritator-tot," she shot back, grateful to stop thinking about Dylan. "You're not the only one who's —"

"Scared? Nervous? Petrified that Uncle Devious has got some skanky plan up his lumberjack sleeve to involve

Dylan in our doings?" Alex took a deep breath. "Look, Cam — like it or not — we just have to deal. We had no choice in the timing of this mother-and-child reunion."

Alex let Cam pedal ahead of her. She knew she was being totally irrational, but suddenly, every little thing about her twin annoyed her. The way her pink jacket puffed just so, the way she leaned forward on her pricey, ergonomically correct mountain bike. The fact that she'd been brought up wealthy and carefree — while Alex had scrounged in poverty, often feeling lonely, different, and desperate.

She thought about Sara's funeral — and remembered what Karsh had said about her mother. She'd thought he meant Sara, but later realized that it had been Miranda he was speaking of. "I knew her. She was quite a babe. Stellar eyes she had, like your own."

Alex had written "scripts" in her head. She'd choreographed and even imagined the music for the scene about to be played out. Sample dialogue [Comedy]: Alex: "What took ya' so long, Moms?" Miranda: "Ooops, never checked the clock." Or [Drama]: Alex: "How could you abandon us?" Miranda: "I had no choice. I was kidnapped." Or [Musical]: Alex: "You say you're my real mom? Prove it." Which was when Miranda would sing a blues number about leaving, never to be seen again.

In some peculiar way, Alex liked this last scenario

best. Because it would vindicate her allegiance to Sara — to date, her best and only mom.

Cam now led the way, bouncing her bike off a curb and steering through the ornate entrance arch to Mariner's Park. They hesitated before hopping off their bikes to begin walking toward the hill.

It was when they began to hike up the familiar narrow path that they instinctively reached out to each other and clasped hands. And traded telepathic "what-if's."

What if she doesn't like us? Cam wondered.

What if we don't like her? Alex proposed.

What if she does some weird spell on us and spirits us away? Cam fretted.

What if she only likes one of us? Alex mused.

What if there's no connection at all? Cam speculated.

"Hello," Alex challenged out loud, "what if she doesn't even show? If this is all a Thantos move to lure us here, away from home, so he or some of his shady associates can snare us?"

"No," Cam said passionately. "I believe him, Als. She'll be there."

"Is that your mojo, your heart's desire, or your deepest fear talking?" her sister challenged.

"Is that your paranoia or your pessimism asking?" Cam shot back.

It was still dark, windy, and cold in the park. Cam hitched up the collar of her pink ski parka.

Alex buttoned the camouflage jacket she'd worn over her sweatshirt. "Remember the last time we wore these?" she asked as they neared the huge, gnarled tree.

"Fiasco," Cam remembered. "It was the night we did the Transporter and wound up in different places —"

"And Ileana forbade us to ever use the spell again."

"Hey, I've still got some stuff in my pocket." Cam held out her palm but Alex ignored it. She was straining through the darkness, squinting up at the tree, which was still yards away.

"It's mugwort or marjoram," Cam was jabbering, "the herbs we used. And look at this — I've still got Ileana's crystal."

"I don't think she's there," Alex said. "Our . . . you know, Miranda. I'm not getting anything but regular cold-night park smells and noises."

Cam focused her laser-sharp vision on the ancient twisted tree, peering into its familiar crevices and towering branches. "There's no one there, but the sun's not up yet, either."

"I told you, she's a no-show, by choice or by Thantos's trickery," Alex whispered. "Or maybe it's all one huge scam — and the joke's on us."

Cam didn't answer. She was staring now at a thin

ribbon of light glowing behind the hill. The dawning sun, breathtaking and pink, framed the twisted silhouette of the tree where they were to meet their mother.

"Look." Cam squeezed her sister's hand.

"I know. And there's the moon." They looked behind them. The pale moon was fading in a slowly lightening sky.

"Pine needles," Alex murmured. "And lavender. Can you smell that?" She closed her eyes and inhaled deeply. "Pine and lavender and . . . rosemary."

Cam's shoulders hunched involuntarily inside her pink parka. Her grip on Alex's hand tightened. She was afraid to turn around, to look back at the tree . . . at the person she now knew was standing there.

But who? Had Thantos lured them into a trap? Or was it finally really her? Cam's heart thudded.

She didn't want to admit it — especially not now — that it was easier for her to face the possibility of deadly danger than the likelihood that their mother had come to meet them.

Still, neither of them turned to see who was there.

It was a moment frozen in time. When it passed, their lives would never be the same again.

CHAPTER EIGHT
MIRANDA

"Artemis? Apolla?"

The voice was soft, whispery, the same voice they'd heard the first time their necklaces bonded, the voice they'd heard on the phone. But so near, so fragile, light enough to ride the early morning breeze, to caress their cheeks, to brush their lips.

Tears burst from Alex's silver-gray eyes. Cam was hyperventilating. In slo-mo and in sync, they turned around.

Alex had pictured a sidelined super-woman, a fierce witch of wondrous powers.

Cam had visualized Miranda as gentle, calm, and loving, nervous about meeting them.

The stranger who stood before them was all and none of that.

She was a replica of them, as if a computer had projected what they'd look like in twenty-five years. But it was more than the metallic gray eyes, irises outlined in black; more than the full lips, prominent cheekbones, and chestnut hair. Her emotions too, seemed to mirror theirs, everything they were feeling — anticipation, anxiety, even terror — her face reflected back.

That was the moment Cam and Alex knew it was actually happening. She was real and she was here. And no matter what they were about to find out, they had at least . . . at last . . . seen their mother. And it was going to be okay.

If this had been a movie, Alex found herself thinking, this would have been the moment they ran toward one another, embraced tightly, cried profusely, forgave and forgot, then walked off into the sunset, arms around one another's shoulders.

But this was real life, and it was dawn, and their new beginning was unscripted.

Tentatively, they stepped toward each other.

Miranda's expression changed. Cam now saw a mixture of awe and relief on the face that belonged to a stranger, yet looked so much like her own. Awe and relief and a joy so profound it frightened both of them.

"Artemis?" the woman called out tentatively.

Cam shook her head. "I'm Camr — I'm Apolla," she said.

"I'm Artemis." The trapped words now escaped Alex's dry mouth.

"Oh." Miranda's eyes glimmered as they searched Alex's face. "I thought, maybe, because you were crying, I thought you were . . ." She smiled now, at a memory etched in her brain. "When you were newborns, Artemis clutched her tiny fists and turned red with rage, but never cried. Apolla was placid and calm. I imagined she would become the more emotional one —"

"I never cry." For some dumb reason, Alex needed to be sure this woman — Miranda — knew that about her.

"But she still goes red with rage," Cam offered. "And I'm still the calm one."

Right, Alex silently contradicted, *that's why you're shaking and sweating.*

Miranda cocked her head; a faint smile played on her lips.

"You heard that?" Cam asked slowly, awestruck.

"It's one of the very few gifts I have left," she explained quietly, "And even that one is . . . undependable."

Alex heard her swallow, heard every beat of this

woman's heart pounding, in a rhythm that matched her own.

"Does that mean you —" Alex started

"Have no powers? I mean, you used to, right?" Cam stammered, "That's what they told us."

"They used to tell me that twins finished each other's sentences. I didn't think I'd ever see that for myself." The yearning, in her eyes, and in her voice, was palpable.

It seemed to let loose a string of soul-baring questions, hopes, fears, accusations. Words tumbled in free fall, long-harbored feelings so raw, finally expressed. Because all three spoke at the same time, their words intertwined, one overlaying the next, the beginning of one person's sentences ending with the question mark of another's.

A tape of the confused conversion would have sounded like this —

"I can't believe it's really you!" "Why didn't you come looking for us?" "I thought I'd never see you again." "How could you leave us?" "Didn't you want us?" "How could you not know we were alive?" "Have you been happy?" "Has someone been taking care of you, loving you?" "I never stopped thinking of you, I never thought this moment would really come — I never thought I'd find you . . ." "I've been waiting all my life . . ."

Miranda got in the last words, and they hung in the air. "I thought I'd killed you." She began to weep, her frail body convulsed in wracking sobs. She made no motion to cover up her agony. Tears rushed down her face in torrents.

Alex and Cam made for her, but stopped suddenly only inches away, afraid to touch her.

Seeing their bewildered faces, Miranda forced herself to stop crying. She lifted her chin, almost defiantly. That was when a small window to her soul cracked open — and her daughters could see the tiniest spark of who she had been, and might one day be again — proud and fierce, childlike in some ways, maternal and nurturing in others.

Calmly, Miranda looked from Alex to Cam. And said, so matter-of-factly that their jaws dropped, "I'd like to hug you now."

The twins lost it. Laughing at the wildly impulsive request, or command, for it sounded like both, crying because they could finally give into their lost-child-found dreams, they fell into Miranda's outstretched arms, and pressed themselves to her.

As Alex inhaled the mingled scents of rosemary and lavender, the sweet sting of pine, the fear that she could never accept anyone but Sara as her mother, faded; didn't matter. Fierce love and loyalty for one did nothing to diminish the intensity of her feelings for the other.

Holding Miranda tightly, Cam knew what Alex was feeling.

She wished she could feel it, too.

She'd been born to this woman, had lived inside her, their hearts had once beat in the same body. But now, Cam's heart had a mind of its own. It belonged to Emily. And while she and Alex clung to Miranda, Cam knew she could not, would never, betray the woman who loved and reared her.

If Miranda knew how torn Camryn felt, she didn't let on. Nor did Cam break their embrace.

Refusing to let go of one another, exhausted and exhilarated, they sat on the dewy ground with Miranda between them. Alex's head rested on the quilt that lay across her shoulders; Cam let her hand slip into Miranda's.

They attempted only a few questions, offered only what answers they could manage right now. There'd be time, the rest of their lives, they hoped, to ask and answer and maybe even understand, all the others.

Cam and Alex came away knowing that Miranda's meltdown the day of their birth, the day Aron was murdered, had left her so broken, so helpless, that she had accepted Fredo DuBaer's terrible lie — that her infant twins were also dead. Thantos had never contradicted his brother. Only recently had he given Miranda the miraculous "news" — her daughters were alive, found and together.

Miranda assumed Thantos had not known that before.

"How could you believe him?" Alex challenged. "He had you locked away, like a prisoner."

"No," Miranda protested. "He took care of me. The place, Rolling Hills . . . being there probably saved my life."

Alex rejected the notion, and said so; Cam wavered, unsure of what to believe.

They were too terrified to ask what she'd meant before when she said, "I thought I'd killed you." And when Miranda didn't open that door again, Cam and Alex were content to leave it shut.

Miranda was relieved that her daughters had been cared for, loved, cherished. Not only by the protectors Karsh had found for them, but by Karsh himself. She was, however, surprised to learn that Ileana was their guardian. "Thantos's daughter, Ileana?" she'd asked.

Which first shocked and horrified the twins. Knowing how the haughty young witch hated the black-bearded tracker, their hearts ached for Ileana.

"When Thantos found out you were alive," Miranda continued, "he told me he watched you for a while —"

More like stalked, Cam thought, then quickly squashed the words, hoping Miranda hadn't overheard.

Alex lifted her head from Miranda's shoulder. "What else did he tell you?" she asked warily.

"That you had accepted your destiny —"

"Our destiny?" Alex asked.

"To be witches, you mean?" Cam said.

Miranda's eyes swept their faces, wondering, asking, but not in a language Alex could make sense of. "Yes, to be witches," she finally said. "That and more. I understand that your skills at the craft are exceptional."

"Did Thantos tell you that, too?" Alex wanted to know.

"He confirmed it. Your friend Brianna told me, though not in those words." She turned to Cam. "She said Apolla — she called you Camryn, of course — had 'mojo.'"

"And what'd she say about me, that I was just plain weird?" Alex asked.

"She said you gave her the creeps," Miranda announced proudly.

Cam ducked her head fast, so that her twin couldn't see her face, but Alex heard her sister's stifled laughter. Ignoring her, she asked Miranda, "So what now? I mean . . . this is so . . . so —"

"Weird," Cam chimed in, "but, you know, amazing." Suddenly, she wanted this to be over. "Do you have to go back to Rolling Hills?" she blurted.

All at once, guiltily, she realized that she'd been worrying about Dylan, about her upset parents, and that she'd harbored a secret hope that Miranda might magically be able to help straighten things out. Protect Dyl, if necessary, from Thantos. The weight of that hope and the revelation that their birth mother could barely help herself seemed to have exhausted Cam. She felt tired. She wanted to go home.

"Rolling Hills?" Miranda had been considering the question. "No," she said finally. "I had thought —" She shook her head and smiled. This time the smile was heavy with sighs and sadness. "Ah, but now that I know . . ." Miranda cleared her throat and began again, sounding more upbeat. "Now that I've seen for myself that you're safe . . . and well cared for, I'm going back to Coventry Island."

Alex asked, "Is Thantos coming to take you there? Because, you know, we can . . . you can come with us to Cam's house and —"

Cam paled. "— Which would be great, but this isn't the best time," she reminded Alex.

Miranda shook her head. "No, it isn't the best time. For any of us. Not yet." I want to be part of your lives. But we . . . *I,*" she corrected herself. "I'm not ready. I would like to go home — home to Coventry Island — to build up my strength and renew my skills, to become the mother you —" *Want,* she almost said, but changed it to: "— *deserve.* And to give you . . . to give us time."

Without warning, Miranda laughed. "Of course, I've no way of arranging it. Your uncle brought me here — and I think he thought I would be staying. Once, I could have transported myself. No longer —"

"We can help you," Alex blurted all at once. "Can't we, Cam? You still have the mugwort and quartz crystal —"

"The Transporter?" Miranda said, as surprised that she remembered the name of the spell as she was that her children could perform it. "But have you been initiated yet?" their mother asked, confused. She reached down and picked up the quilt. "The Transporter is not fledgling-level magick —"

"We've got mojo," Cam said.

"And good genes," Alex added.

Miranda smiled gratefully. "And this," she said, handing them the faded patchwork coverlet. "Each of these panels I filled with herbs, to comfort and protect you. They're old now, dry and musty, but they may still carry their purpose and mine."

Alex gently took the quilt. Burying her face in its fragrant folds, she inhaled deeply.

Working from memory, and somewhat hidden beneath the thick, low branches of the oak tree, Cam inscribed a circle in the earth around Miranda. After putting the quilt in the basket of her bicycle, Alex marked the compass points with stones instead of candles.

Their mother stood within the boundary, watching them, delighted, impressed.

Cam sprinkled the herbs she'd found in her pocket inside the circle, then she rubbed the crystal, while Alex began to recite the spell.

"Wait," Cam cried suddenly. "We will see you again, won't we?"

"Whenever you need or want me near. Count on it," the gentle witch promised.

Alex found her voice. "What should we . . . call you?"

Not Mom, Cam thought. *I can't, I'm not ready.*

Alex dittoed the sentiment.

"How about Miranda?" their mother asked. "Does that work for you? And I will try to remember you're not Apolla and Artemis anymore, but Camryn and Alexandra."

"Miranda," Alex tested it, in a tone half grudging, half shy. "I . . . We're . . . I'm glad you came —"

Miranda laughed at some private joke — and then, standing inside the circle Cam had set down, she shared it: "I'm sorry I was late," she said.

Alex laughed.

"*Good magick,*" Cam prompted, elbowing her sister.

"*Like air and water flow . . . Transport Miranda,*" Alex chanted.

"*Transport her body and spirit now,*" Cam said.

A breeze stirred the branches above them. Below,

Cam noticed a jogger chasing his cap, a woman's scarf fluttering wildly, the long hair of a golden retriever bristling in the wind.

Alex felt the cold gust invade her clothing, heard the wind hiss and stir wet leaves in lifeless heaps, heard the clacking of dead branches, then a far-off rumble like a warning of thunder. She covered her ears as the squall picked up, circling her, whirling bits of paper and dead leaves and clods of earth. Cam shut her eyes against the stinging swirl.

The storm roared and then subsided.

The circle in which Miranda had stood was empty.

CHAPTER NINE
A THREAT REALIZED

There was a police car in the driveway of Cam and Alex's house.

A small crowd had gathered.

Dave was talking to one of the officers.

Along with a worried neighbor, a second cop was trying to comfort Emily, who was sitting on the front steps, crying.

Miranda, Alex thought. Were the police looking for her? Had she escaped from the clinic rather than been released? Was this another trick of Thantos's — to give them a "taste" of their mother, then call the police to have her put away again? Was she considered dangerous? Even as these possibilities crossed her mind, Alex rejected them.

Cam cut through her sister's panicked musing with one word: *Dylan!* They dropped their bikes. Alex whisked up Miranda's quilt, and they ran toward the house.

"Is that them?" the policeman asked Dave.

"Yes," Dave said, hurrying across the lawn to them.

Emily stood up too fast. The second officer, a short, strong woman, caught her as she stumbled backward.

"Are you all right? Where were you?" Dave demanded.

"We . . . took a ride," Alex answered lamely.

"Over to Mariner's Park. What happened?" Cam watched the officer and their neighbor ease Emily down onto the steps again. "Is Mom all right?"

Mom. The word came so easily, so rightfully. The amazing woman in the park had given birth to them, but Emily Barnes had been Cam's mother for fifteen years!

"How do you think she is?" Dave demanded. "Where's Dylan?"

The twins looked at each other.

What are we supposed to say, in a Dumpster? Cam silently asked Alex.

No way, her sister argued.

"Dylan," Dave repeated. "Where is he? Was he with you?"

"No," Cam blurted. "He's probably in —"

"Trouble, right?" Alex cut her off. "I mean, if he

doesn't get home fast. Uh, last time I saw him, he was in his room. I spoke to him —"

"When?" Emily came over, steadied by the police-woman.

"Last night. Just before we went to PITS."

And about five minutes before that hulking maniac Thantos broke into our room, Cam silently wailed.

"Did he seem disturbed, angry?" the policewoman asked.

"Well, yeah —" Alex looked at Dave.

"As we told you," Dave said, "we gave him a dressing-down last night — about his skipping some classes at school, spending too much time on his computer and not enough on homework. Nothing radical. Nothing to warrant this —"

"The window in his room was open," Emily said shakily. "You see, I went in early this morning —"

"At the crack of dawn," Dave explained. "After last night's scene, she couldn't sleep."

"And he wasn't there. He hadn't been to bed at all. The window was wide open and the blinds were rattling." Emily was wringing her hands. "Dylan's computer was on. The screensaver was flashing — the one with the snowboarding scenes. But he wasn't there. So I went into the girls' room —"

"And they were out, too," Dave took over. "But at least we knew they'd slept there —"

"Dylan's window was open?" Cam asked.

"And his backpack and ski jacket were gone." Emily's eyes teared up again. "We called everyone we could think of. And unless his friends are lying —"

"Which I don't believe they are," Dave assured the policewoman. "We haven't a clue as to where he is or what kind of trouble he may be in."

"So you were the last to see him, Alexandra?" The other officer had joined them.

"I'm Camryn."

"Yeah," Alex said, clutching the quilt with its faded fragrances and colors. "I guess."

"And you had no reason to think he was planning to run away?"

"Run away? Dylan? No way," Alex insisted.

"That's what I told them. Dylan's not like that. He wouldn't have crept out a window." Impulsively, Emily took Alex's hand. "You know him, he'd have walked out the front door and slammed it behind him. I . . . I felt almost relieved when I saw that you two were gone as well. I thought you were all together."

Emily patted and released Alex's hand and turned to Cam. "I tried to reach you. I called your cell phone number. But it was here, in your bag, in your room. I couldn't believe you'd leave it behind."

Dave ran a hand through his thick dark curls. "And not leave us a note." He stared hard at the twins. "Do you have any ideas?" he asked. "A premonition, a hunch, anything?"

The images returned to Cam, the ones Thantos had created so vividly. As Dave and Emily went inside with the police, Cam envisioned the Dumpster again. It was parked behind a store. *The Cand . . . on* was written on the iron box in fading letters. *The Cand . . . on —*

Got it! Alex hollered. *The Cand-le Connecti-on,* she told her sister.

"Yes!" Cam exclaimed. The Candle Connection was a franchise peddling every kind, size, fragrance, and color candle under the sun — towering pillars, floating flowers, beeswax, dripless, round, square, triangular, animal- and vegetable-shaped candles, tapers, and tea lights, plus lacy sachets, scented oils, bath beads. They hawked candles the way the Colonel sold chicken. There were at least eight of them in a ten-mile radius of Marble Bay. One of them was right downtown.

"But with all that's going on, can we leave now?" Cam asked her sister.

"Let's see. Today is Sunday. No trash pickup." Alex

pretended to weigh the options. "Tomorrow's Monday. Guess we can wait till tomorrow when the garbage truck shows up —"

Remembering that iron-jawed assassin was all Cam needed. "You made your point," she said. "I vote for now."

They were heading for the sidewalk where they'd left their bikes when two things happened at once to change their plans.

One: Jason Weissman pulled up. Tall, dark, and crazy for Cam, the hottie who'd once worked at PITS had been cruising by and seen the small crowd breaking up and the police car in the Barneses' driveway. In response to his concerned "What's up?" Cam wondered if he could give them a lift to The Candle Connection.

Alex rolled her eyes, knowing the boy would give them a lift to the moon if Cam offered him the honor.

Two: As they wheeled their no-longer-needed bikes back to the garage, Alex's extraordinary hearing and sense of smell went into overdrive. At first she thought it was the quilt she'd flung over her shoulder that was giving off the distinctive sharp scents. Then she realized that someone was hiding in the shrubbery that separated the Barneses' property from their neighbor's, someone who smelled of jasmine and fear.

"Whoops, we'd better tell my parents we're taking off," Cam said. "They're freaked enough."

"No probs. You go with Jason. I'll hang around and let them know you're okay."

"And?" Cam asked suspiciously.

"Busted," Alex conceded. "Before you take off, could you kind of subtly focus your outstanding orbs into the bushes and tell me who's crouching there?"

Cam spun around.

"Oh, that was casual," Alex grumbled.

Her twin scarcely heard her. *It's a girl.* Cam sent a mind message. *The one who came to school all beat up —*

"Kenya Carson?" Alex whispered. "The kid your crew was talking about at PITS? She's supposed to be in Dylan's class, right?"

What is she doing here? Cam marveled. *Why is she hiding?*

CHAPTER TEN
HIDE-AND-SEEK

The girl who stood in front of Alex seemed nothing like the spunky snowboarder chick who occasionally freestyled with Dylan and his bud Robbie Meeks.

Chewing on her nails, brown eyes darting frantically, Kenya wasn't as bruised and jumpy as she'd been a week ago. Which was when she'd showed up at school telling one person that a bad day on the slopes was responsible for her black eye, scraped knee, and chipped tooth, and swearing to another that she'd tripped on the stairs.

She was having the same get-it-straight trouble today.

She said she'd come by to see Dylan and that finding a police car in the driveway had totally freaked her. She didn't know why she'd ducked behind the bushes, she just did.

Fair enough. Maybe she was afraid the cops would take one look at her and arrest her parents, Alex thought, remembering Kristen's child abuse rant. She could buy that.

What set Alex's alarm ringing were Kenya's dumb answers to what she'd wanted to see Dylan about. Ranging from "I don't know" to "borrowing a book" to "homework help," the jittery girl couldn't lie and look Alex in the eye at the same time.

"Run that by me again," Alex suggested.

"Okay, okay. I just wanted to catch him before —" Kenya stopped and switched from nail-gnawing to lip-nibbling. "Not *before,*" she corrected herself. "I mean, I just needed to talk to him, you know?"

"Not really." Alex cocked her head and listened intently.

Kenya's brain was a babble of fears, excuses, questions, and pain. Alex was having a hard time cutting through the hysterical mess to find out what the wigged-out girl was really thinking. She'd caught one complete sentence — *How could anyone think my parents did this to me?* — when a weird click-clacking noise broke her concentration.

Alex glanced over at the police cruiser.

Did the cops have a laptop? Were they using some handheld computer device? The officers weren't even in their car, Alex realized; they were still inside with Dylan's panicked parents. She looked up at the blond boy's window, half expecting to see him at his desk, hunched over his PC. But he was gone. MIA. And probably in bigger trouble than Emily and Dave could imagine.

So who was tapping on a keyboard? "Can you hear that?" she asked Kenya.

"What?" the flipped girl asked.

"A computer," Alex said. "Someone's on a computer —"

Kenya went ashen. "He told you," she cried. "Dag, I can't believe it."

"Who told me what?" Alex asked.

But Kenya, bandaged knee, sore cheek, bruised eye, and all, tore out of there without another word.

Alex hoped Cam was having better luck.

Not so far.

Cam and Jason had checked out three different Candle Connection locations and hadn't found a Dumpster that matched the one Thantos had shown the twins.

"I don't get it," Jason said after the third stop. "I

mean, I know you get these wild hunches. And you said your brother mentioned a Dumpster. But how do you know it wasn't that green one we saw behind The Candle Connection on Pierce Street?"

"Um, because . . ." Cam tried to come up with something believable. "That one was . . . plastic," she mumbled as they pulled up behind The Candle Connection superstore in the mall outside of Salem.

She didn't say that she'd developed a reverse game of hot-or-cold, that at the earlier sites, she'd felt a dull warmth, but that as they'd approached this mall, her hands and feet had felt strangely icy. And that now as they pulled into the parking lot at the back of the buildings, chills were rattling through her.

"It's h-here," she managed to stammer.

"Where?" Jason asked, scanning the lot.

"You must have passed it," Cam told the confused boy. "Go back."

Jason did a U-ee and headed back in the direction they'd come from.

"There it is!" Shivering, Cam was hugging herself, staring at the gray metal Dumpster hidden from view behind piles of boxes. "Over there. See — there's the store."

Jason could see The Candle Connection sign on the

warehouse-sized building but not the Dumpster, the massive iron box with its half-worn-away logo. But, following Cam's directions, he parked near the trash, then watched, scratching his handsome, dark-haired head, as she bolted from his car and raced through an obstacle course of refuse behind the store.

Shaking with cold, Cam scaled the hill of rubble hiding the Dumpster and peered down into the box. At first, almost relieved, she saw nothing important. Huge green plastic bags surrounded by bubble wrap, wrapping paper, bottles, and cardboard cartons.

Then a bit of twinkling gold metal caught her eye. She telescoped in on the object.

There, wedged between a plastic bag and a collapsed carton, was Dylan's earring.

Her heart froze. Was she too late? Had her brother already been mashed by the iron jaws of the truck? Was Dyl fill — as in landfill?

Cam climbed into the Dumpster and scrambled to retrieve her brother's earring.

"Are you okay? He's not in there, is he?" Jason called breathlessly. He'd run over the moment she'd disappeared from sight. "Camryn, answer me!"

"No, he's not here," she said, climbing out, holding up the tiny gold earring, "but he was."

*   *   *

Jason dropped her off at home.

Alex was in the kitchen, preparing a cup of tea. "For Emily," she explained. "She's a mess. So," she asked anxiously, "anything?"

Cam noticed Miranda's quilt slung like a shawl over Alex's shoulders. "It just feels good," her sister dismissed her questioning glance. "I didn't get much out of Kenya. She was, like, radically unhinged. And then I said the magic word *computer* and — *poof!* — she took off. Cam, what happened? What's the matter?"

Cam held out Dylan's earring.

Alex threw down the tea bag she'd been dunking and hurried to her twin. "Where did you get that?"

"It was in the Dumpster, Als." Cam was shaking. "The Dumpster Thantos showed us."

Alex took off the fragrant, faded quilt and wrapped Cam in it. "Let's go upstairs," she said softly but firmly. There was no thought of sharing this stunning info with parents or police. The news, Alex pointed out, was way beyond weird and would require even weirder explanations. Plus, Cam believed, the less Dave and Emily knew about the twins' witchy powers, the safer her adoptive 'rents would be.

All they had to do was find and rescue Dylan before it was too late.

If it wasn't too late already.

"We need help. We've got to find Dylan," Cam said, climbing the stairs, feeling slightly warmer and less frantic huddled in the quilt. "Got any ideas?"

"Nine-one-one Karsh and Ileana again. Give them another heads-up," Alex suggested. "Call in the Coventry cavalry."

CHAPTER ELEVEN
WHAT A FOOL BELIEVES

There was so much to put down. His bony knees knocked against the top drawer of his desk. Karsh hunched over and wrote fiercely, attacking his notebook as if he had to hold it down, force the words into it before it sprang shut. He wrote and wrote in his cramped, precise script, filling up pages as quickly as he could.

Putting it all down on paper, or parchment in his case, was Karsh's backup plan.

The family secrets he had to reveal, he had hoped to do in person. He didn't want Ileana to discover them as harshly as she'd discovered that Thantos was her father. The pages Karsh was filling would affect the rest of her life — and Camryn's and Alexandra's. They contained nothing less than their destiny.

But was recording the past more urgent than the present? Camryn and Alexandra had called out for help.

He had heard them, of course, but could not go to them — not now, not with so little time left. He might, however, be able to locate Dylan for them through the use of his stones. Reluctantly, he set down his pen and gathered his magick stones.

The old warlock was dismayed to find only four of the sacred five left. Intuitively, he realized that Tsuris had stolen one — the African tigereye, which might still have Ileana's imprint on it. He shuddered to think what the ruffian sons of Fredo might do to her.

Hastily, Karsh assembled the remaining rocks — substituting a large raw topaz for the lost stone — and sought Dylan.

He found the blond boy wandering alone, limping, and lost in the woods. Although his head still ached from where it had hit the slate floor, Karsh forced himself to focus on the flora and fauna around the injured child. Then, by a process of elimination, and consulting his botanical books, he narrowed the area to New England and determined, as much by instinct as geography, that it was near Salem, graveyard of so many of their ancestors.

Karsh shivered as he thought of one of them, the

one he'd been writing about — the young healer Abigail Antayus, who had been turned in by a jealous warlock for practicing witchcraft. And hanged from the oak tree in what was now called Mariner's Park.

Karsh leaned back to catch his breath before contacting the twins. His eye fell on his parchment notebook. An uncomfortable thought struck him. What if time ran out before he could tell Ileana what she needed to know? What if she never got to read all he had written?

No, he knew her. He would find a way to be sure she — and no one else — found his book.

Karsh felt lighter, freer. The burden of carrying so many secrets for so very long had been heavier than he'd thought.

A knock at the door startled him — although it was soft, gentle; clearly not Tsuris and Vey again, nor impulsive Ileana. Karsh frowned. He wasn't expecting company and he wasn't quite done writing. With some annoyance, he pushed his chair back, pulled a book out of the bookcase, and hid his notebook inside its hollowed-out pages. Quickly, he returned it to the shelf.

Another knock. Striding toward the front door, he hesitated for a moment. He felt a female presence there, caught a scent of lavender.

His fall must have rattled his brain, for only in a

dream could the woman he'd pictured be outside his cottage. He opened the door, and his jaw fell in shock.

Wildly, incomprehensibly, he saw Camryn or Alexandra . . . many years in the future. Or was it the ghost of someone he'd once known?

Her eyes, the same charcoal-rimmed gray he'd looked into so many times before, searched his. Her hair, tied back in a long braid, was a gray-flecked version of the chestnut color he remembered.

But it was only when she reached out, touched his arm, and whispered his name softly, did Karsh know this was no dream, no vision of the future or apparition from the past. Here and now, alive and real, stood Miranda DuBaer. Long missing, feared dead. Found.

Karsh couldn't find his voice. In the same moment, they stepped toward each other and embraced. Karsh closed his eyes and, pressing her to his cheek, inhaled deeply. Sweet lavender, crisp rosemary, the fresh scent of young pine trees. His eyes welled with tears. "Oh, child," he whispered. "Dear Miranda."

"This room looks exactly as I remember it." Miranda settled on Karsh's comfortable but threadbare sofa and looked around. "As if time stood still . . ."

Karsh sat next to her and took her still-smooth hands in his lined, weathered ones. "As if," he echoed, staring in a disbelief that was slowly warming to pure delight.

"What's happened to you?" Miranda asked, gently touching the purpling bruise on the side of his head.

Karsh flinched.

"It must be recent," Miranda noted, "and still painful."

The spot where his head had hit the slate when Tsuris shoved him down was swollen and tender. Karsh suspected it was the cause of the sporadic blurriness and loss of concentration he was having. Normally, he'd have gone to the clinic, but he hadn't wanted to waste the time.

"It's only a bruise," Karsh said. "There are other, more important wounds to heal."

Miranda's eyes glinted with excitement as she answered Karsh's unspoken question. "I've seen them. My babies. Apolla and Artemis."

A warm smile lit Karsh's face. "Then you've seen how wonderfully, how beautifully they're turning out." Immediately, he regretted saying that. What if Miranda misunderstood? If she took it to mean they'd done fine without her?

"I don't think that," she responded, reading his mind again — one of the few skills she seemed not to have lost. "I'm proud of them and so very grateful for all you've done. It couldn't have been easy."

Karsh was about to explain that Ileana deserved much credit, but just then Miranda cocked her head in a way that instantly took him back. She'd always been a bit mischievous. "I'd bet Artemis — Alexandra — is a handful."

"Takes after her mother," Karsh rejoined. And then he couldn't stop himself. "Dear Miranda. What happened? We thought you were dead!"

"There were times, days, months when I wished for that," Miranda admitted. "My Aron murdered, our children gone . . ."

Karsh lifted her chin. "How much do you remember?"

"Not much. The joy of the twins' birth — and then you coming in and telling me Aron was gone."

"Nothing else?" Karsh queried.

"I think Fredo spoke to me after you left. It's been so long now. I don't know what I remember and what I've been told." She looked up at him pleadingly. "Tell me."

Karsh sighed. "You asked me to take the babies. You were wild with grief and fear. You wanted a moment alone. I didn't think it wise in your distraught state but I left nevertheless. When I returned, you were gone, Miranda. Just gone. We found safe havens for the twins and then searched everywhere, the whole of Coventry, for you. Days turned to weeks, weeks to months . . ." He trailed off.

"I wish I could fill in the blanks for you, but I can't," Miranda admitted.

"But at some point," he pressed, "you knew you had a home, a family. Why didn't you contact us? So many years . . ."

Her eyes filled with tears. She shook her head helplessly. "So much to explain, my old friend. And so much to learn. Do we have time?"

She had always been extraordinarily intuitive, Karsh thought. He sprang from the couch. "You must be hungry. I'll find some food, brew some tea." He turned from her so that his face wouldn't betray him. "Dear Miranda," he promised, "we have as much time as we need."

And so they talked. Earnestly, wholeheartedly, regretful of the years lost, joyful at the new day that had come. Long into the afternoon they talked.

Although Thantos had told her some, Miranda wanted to hear from the trusted elder, the oldest survivor of the Antayus clan, how her babies really were. Karsh guided her through the years she'd missed, detailing with pride all the twins had accomplished, all the potential they displayed. He was most proud of the people they were becoming: vital, strong, funny, loving, loyal, and dedicated to helping those in need of their gifts.

The missing years were harder for Miranda to explain. She'd been told she'd gone mad, then catatonic, fallen into a kind of coma —

"Told by whom?" Karsh asked, then felt ill, uneasy, because he realized it was Thantos who'd informed — or misinformed — her. "So he knew, all this time, you were alive."

"He told me the babies were gone," Miranda continued.

"He said they were dead?" Now Karsh was truly incredulous. "How dare —"

"He didn't use that word." She shook her head. "He said they'd been stolen, taken away. He said he would find them if it was the last thing he ever did."

Truer than she knew, thought Karsh bitterly.

"When the years went by and there was no sign of them, I accepted . . . the inevitable," Miranda continued. "I had many breakdowns. I lost all of my powers — some never returned."

The look on Miranda's face stopped Karsh from telling her the harsh truth. He turned away to make it more difficult for her to break into his thoughts — which were that Thantos, whom she clearly trusted, had lied to her and kept up the ruse for fifteen years.

Oh, Thantos had been trying to find the twins, all right. To trick them, lure them into believing in his righteousness, to turn them away from all their father had believed and stood for.

Miranda had been the bait.

Ileana believed that if Thantos did not succeed in swaying his nieces, making them trust and follow him, that, sooner or later, he would have them killed. Karsh had not been so sure. He was now.

But this was not the time to confide his fears to Miranda. Not while she was still weak, unsure of herself, and without the powerful magick that had been her birthright. For now, Karsh decided, it was better for her to believe what she'd been told all these years.

He fished for something positive to say. He took her hands and looked into her eyes. "You return at the right moment, Miranda. Your children will soon be preparing for their initiation. They need a true mother now."

Miranda shook her head sadly. "No. I'm not ready. I can't."

"Your powers will return," Karsh promised. "Count on it."

"Until they do —" She lifted her chin in the same defiant way Alexandra often did. "I deem myself an unfit mother. Until they can trust me — and I can trust myself. So I ask you to keep protecting them, to continue as their guardian."

Karsh pursed his lips. Well, there was one thing he

could be honest about. "It isn't I who have protected them. That job was given to —"

The door banged open, interrupting him. "Faithless, feeble old fool!" Her cape flaring, her face red with rage, she charged wildly into his cottage. "Karsh!" she shouted. "My home has been trashed! Why weren't you checking on it? How could you let this happen?"

Karsh turned to Miranda. "May I introduce your daughters' true guardian, Ileana."

For the first time since she'd swung in, Ileana saw who was there. She stunned herself by falling to her knees. "Miranda?" the hot-tempered young witch gasped. Then she lost sight of the spectral woman as tears, the first she'd shed since the trial, surfaced like a curtain of mist, blurring everything.

CHAPTER TWELVE
DYLAN'S STING

"Okay, let's review. What do we know?" Alex asked, pacing their room. She stole a glance at her downcast sister, who was leaning against the dresser staring glumly at the earring in her hand.

"We're on our own," Cam said, without looking up. "Bad enough Karsh and Ileana have blown us off. But Miranda —" Cam hadn't been able to get the brief visit from their mother out of her mind. It was ever present. No matter what urgent thoughts she was focused on, Miranda waited just behind them. "I mean, she was nothing like I imagined."

"Oh, give her a break," Alex counseled, trying to

hide her own disappointment and, to tell the truth, a weird kind of satisfaction — because Miranda, beautiful and fragile as she was, offered no contest for Alex's love of Sara. "So she was a little spaced. Who wouldn't be after fifteen years with no one to talk to but the sickos of Rolling Hills —"

"And Uncle Thantos," Cam reminded her, unconsciously tugging the faded quilt more tightly around her shoulders.

"Okay, so where were we?" Alex got back to topic A: "Dylan's gone. But he lost — or possibly left behind on purpose — one of his earrings."

"Wake up and smell the Dumpster," Cam grumbled. "There was nothing 'on purpose' about it. A trail of bread crumbs would've been more helpful."

Alex cast a we-are-so-not-amused glance Cam's way as she paced past her twin for the second time. "Anyway, you found his earring . . . behind The Candle Connection. And that's all we've got to go on. No notes, phone calls, e-mails, or psychic carrier pigeons to announce his whereabouts."

"Only that creepy horror story Uncle Edgar Allan Thantos spun for us." Camryn closed her fist over the precious earring that she used to give her brother grief about. Now she wished she could take it back. Every teasing, taunting, nasty thing she'd ever said to him she'd take back in a flash if he'd just get his skinny, snow-boarding booty home in one piece.

"Oh, and don't forget bush girl — Kenya Carson," Alex remembered. "Did I tell you how fast she split after I mentioned hearing a computer?"

Cam caught a scent of licorice, of anise, one of the herbs Miranda had long ago sewn into the quilt. "Inspiration!" Cam snapped her fingers, unaware of the subtle energies the anise had awakened in her. "Als," she asked, "didn't you say Dyl was e-mailing someone when you walked into his room yesterday?"

"Guy named KC," Alex confirmed.

"Guy?" Cam raised an eyebrow skeptically.

Alex got it. "KC. Kenya Carson!" She slapped her forehead. "Hello, seen my brain? It's never around when I need it."

They rushed toward the connecting bathroom in such sync that they jammed shoulders at the door. "After you," Cam sneered, stepping out of the way. "Did you get to read anything beside those initials? Like what he was saying to her?"

"No, but who says it's too late?" Out of habit, Alex knocked on the door to Dylan's cave.

"Not me," Cam insisted, a sly smile enlivening her defeated face. "Hack much?"

"How hard could it be?" Alex answered, busting into

Dyl's room. "If your everyday dorks, nerds, and hacker-heads can do it, should be a cinch for a couple of determined T'Witches."

It would have been a cinch for anyone. Dylan had left his computer on. His password was stored. When they clicked on his Internet program, all they had to do was hit SIGN ON and there was his e-mail. The message he'd been writing when Alex walked in on him was at the top of his "Sent Mail" file. Addressed to KC, it read: *RideBoy fell for it. I'm meeting him tonight. Same time, same place you did.*

Under "Old Mail," they found Kenya's reply: *Dyl, don't go. Please. He's psycho.*

"That nails it," Alex said, an hour later, when they'd backtracked through Dylan's e-mails and found nothing else to or from KC or about RideBoy. "Time to talk to Kenya."

"But will she talk to us?" Cam asked. "I mean, didn't she do a disappearing act last time you tried?"

"Well, yeah." Alex thought about it.

"I know who she'd talk to," Cam blurted after rubbing her itchy nose on Miranda's quilt.

"Let me guess." Alex's grin was mischievous and triumphant. "Dylan," she said.

Kenya showed up on the button. Fifteen minutes after the dismissal bell rang, anxiously glancing over her shoulder, she climbed the bleachers behind the school and sat down facing the track. As she'd been told to, the nervous girl pulled a book out of her backpack and stared down at it, as if intently reading.

"Hey." A moment later, Alex sat down beside her.

Kenya looked up, surprised, disappointed.

"I'm sorry," she said. "I'm . . . Could you squat somewhere else? I'm meeting somebody."

"He's not coming." Cam, holding a silver-and-black thermal coffee mug, joined them.

"He's not coming because he's gone missing," Alex elaborated, "and you're probably one of the few people who knows where and why."

"But isn't he back?" Kenya asked earnestly. "I mean, I got an e-mail from him last night —" Then she caught Cam's eye. "It wasn't from Dyl, was it?" she asked unhappily.

Cam shook her head. "No, we sent it. We're trying to find him, Kenya."

"So am I!" the girl wailed miserably.

"Cool," said Alex. "Then we're all working together. Who's RideBoy?"

Kenya's bruised brown face went ashen. Instantly, tears flooded her eyes.

Alex handed her a handkerchief. Kenya shook it open and a piece of rock, translucent and faceted like a jewel, fell into her lap. "What's that?" Kenya picked it up and examined it.

"Whoops. How'd that get in there? It's my lucky crystal," Als said. "Hang on to it if you want to."

"Awesome." Kenya clutched the stone, staring at it as if hypnotized. She gasped, startled, when Cam offered her the coffee mug. "It's cocoa," Cam said. "Comfort bev. Go on, have some."

Kenya sniffed at the cup, then took a sip. Her tear-glossed eyes lit with pleasure. "Dag, that flows," she commented. "It's got this weird little kick to it."

"It's all herbal," Cam assured her, drawing out her sun charm.

The "cocoa" and the crystal were having their effect on Kenya. "You guys have any idea what a gnarly champ your bro is?" she raved. "I don't mean just huckin' in the park or, like, boosting in the pipes, I mean, you know, in life totally —"

Zipping her half-moon charm back and forth on her necklace, Alex cautioned, "Yo, don't freak, Kens. Cam and I have this little . . . um, ritual thing we like to do —"

"Actually," Cam jumped in, "it's just reciting a . . . you know, a —"

"Poem," Alex helpfully blurted. "It's called the Truth Inducer."

"*O sun that gives us light and cheer,*" Cam chanted, "*shine through me now to banish fear —*"

"*Free KC from doubt and blame. Let us win her trust,*" Alex said, feeling the heat of her charm ripple through her fingertips, "*and lift her shame.*"

"Dag," Kenya said, impressed. Then she started to tremble. "He's a man, this skanky, like, bald, potbellied creep — not a boy. There's no boy about him. He knows the words, though. Like RideBoy? Ride's a board brand. So I thought he was a kid, like me, like Dyl," she babbled suddenly. "He said he was sixteen!"

Dizzyingly fast, through floods of tears, Kenya's story came out. She'd met a guy who was supposed to be young and snowboard savvy in a chat room on the Net. They wrote back and forth for a couple of weeks, and he said he wanted to meet her.

She knew it was whack to go somewhere private, alone, so she'd insisted on the mall — and he'd agreed, but said it had to be, like, really early on Sunday, 'cause he worked three jobs — one started at six-thirty in the morning and one ended after midnight, and he said he had this weekend gig, and blah, blah, blah.

So they set up to meet at seven-thirty Sunday morning at the big mall outside of Salem.

She was waiting behind The Candle Connection,

where he supposedly worked. And this van he said he'd be driving, this creepy rusty red van, pulled up, and she walked over and this man, this totally old, ugly grown-up, with this funky red knit cap and a disgusting cigarette stink reeking off him, got out and started talking to her.

It took her a minute to get that he was the freak who'd been e-mailing her. He wanted her to get into his van, take a ride with him. And when she said, "No way," he grabbed her arm and tried to shove her into the van. She was hollering, "Let go! Get off of me, you perv!"

And it was Sunday morning. The parking lot was totally empty. No one heard her.

Except him, of course. And he was really twisting her arm hard, so she started really screaming and hammering him. So he threw her down. Hard. He was all, like, "Forget you." But she'd chipped her tooth and gotten all scraped up and she was bleeding. And he just looked at her. And then he got into his van and took off.

She called Dylan from a pay phone. And he called Robbie Meeks, who had his beginner's license, and they drove over and got her. She told them she'd been trying out some new tricks in the parking lot and had wiped out and that some kids had swiped her board.

Robbie bought it. Dylan didn't.

He kept asking her what really happened. Like, for days he was on her about it and finally she told him. And he got so boiling mad he went berserk, but she made him promise not to call the cops or anything; her parents would've killed her. So Dylan decided to handle it himself. He was going to trap RideBoy, set up a sting, a scam to get the creep to meet him.

"I tried to stop him," Kenya cried. "Honest. I tried every day and when he told me it was on, that he had a date to meet the scuzzbucket, I really freaked. I begged him not to. I even went over to your house," she reminded Alex, "but by then, you know, he was gone and the cops were there. And when you said something about a computer, I swear, I thought Dylan had told you what happened. And I was, like, mad at him and scared for him and I didn't know what to do, so I just split."

Alex was patting the anguished girl's back and, although she didn't believe it herself, she kept muttering, "It's okay. It's going to be okay."

Finally, Kenya stopped wailing, snuffled back her tears, and squeezed Alex's hand. "It's all my fault," she said. "I didn't mean to get Dyl all in it. What are you going to do now? I mean, do you know where he is? Do you have, like, any clue?"

Alex was about to say, "No," when she heard Cam moan. Her sister's eyes were shut tight. Palms pressed against her forehead, Cam had begun to shiver.

"Oh, no. What's happening to her?" Kenya squealed,

panicked. "Is she getting sick? Like having a fit or something?"

"No way," Alex said, standing up fast, blocking Cam from Kenya's view. "Probably just had one slab too many of cafeteria mystery meat today. She'll be okay in a second. Oh, and no, we don't know where Dylan is — but we will." She glanced at her sister. "We'll know any minute now."

Suddenly, Alex felt a chill run through her — and heard a rasping voice whispering. She blinked. "Did you just say something?" she asked Kenya. "Did you just . . . like mention some numbers?"

Kenya's brown eyes opened wide.

Alex took a deep breath. "Snap! Gotcha," she told the startled girl, pretending she'd been kidding. "Okay, well, we'll see you." Alex took Cam's arm and helped her up. "Don't worry, Kenya," she said as they left, "everything's going to be all right."

CHAPTER THIRTEEN
A NEW TRICK

"Give!" Alex commanded minutes after they'd left Kenya and started home. "You had a vision, right?"

"Got aspirin?" Cam answered, confirming the guess.

As Alex fished the achy-head med from her backpack, Cam began describing what she'd seen: It wasn't a premonition of the future or a picture from the past. This one was here and now and totally scary. But the image was reassuring at the same time. Because it was of Dylan — and he was alive!

Her blond bro was in a swampy wooded area. The trees were still mostly bare except for the evergreens. On the ground were deep clumps of wet leaves that Dylan was slogging through. He was limping. He looked banged up and lost. His face was so mud-streaked it was hard to see if he'd been cut or bruised. And he was clutching a red knit cap that matched Kenya's description of RideBoy's hat.

"Any clue to where this woodsy swamp might be?" Alex asked.

"Not too far from Marble Bay," Cam said. "I mean the shrubs, pines, and even the iced-over marsh and sandy shoreline looked a lot like around here, but not exactly."

With the slightly bitter remains of the herbal cocoa, Cam downed the aspirins Alex had given her and asked, "What were you saying to Kenya . . . about numbers?"

"The sound track to your movie, I guess," Alex said. "Hot lyrics: 'Seventy degrees, fifty-five minutes, forty-two degrees, thirty minutes.' Never make the Grammys —"

"They're coordinates," Cam said, excited.

"What, like your cashmere turtleneck and peach corduroys?"

"Duh. Latitude and longitude, Als. Got a map?"

While Alex leafed through her geography book, Cam phoned home. Automatically, she asked whether there was any news about Dylan. Emily burst into tears. Dave took the phone. "What? Fine," he said when Cam told him she and Alex were going over to Beth's to study; was it all right if they had supper there? "Aunt Wendy's here and Sally and some of Mom's clients. Just don't be too late," Dave said. "And don't worry. We'll find him."

"Got it!" Alex had flipped to the topographical map of New England. "Check this out." She showed Cam the page. And there they were — the numbers Karsh had whispered to her, latitude and longitude! The coordinates for Salem, Massachusetts, two hours from Marble Bay as the bike pedaled. Shorter as the van flew.

"Dylan must've caught up with RideBoy . . ." Cam conjectured, thinking about the hat.

"And gotten dumped in some deserted place," Alex finished the thought.

"And wouldn't you like to know how to find it — and your gallant brother, too?"

The voice was deep and purringly sarcastic. Spooked, and with the Internet fiend on their minds, the T'Witches whirled, expecting to see RideBoy. Before they knew it, Cam had spun and kicked the predator in the shin. As he bent over, Alex crowned him with her hardcover geography text.

"Oof!" the big, black-bearded man stumbled forward. Only then did Alex catch the odor of spicy cloves, the horse-stable stench of muck, and a scouring sting of ice.

They had attacked their treacherous uncle Lord Thantos.

He moved forward, sweeping them before him into the shade of a giant evergreen. Hidden beneath its thick drooping branches, the giant warlock glared at them. His dark eyes caught Cam's. He stared at her malevolently, whispering hoarsely, his lips barely moving.

All at once Cam's hands and feet felt tight, shrunken, and sharp-toed within her shoes. The same tingling sensation afflicted her hands. When she glanced down at them, her heart nearly leaped from her chest.

In place of her pale, thin fingers were furry gray paws with long sharp nails. Her teeth began to rattle, not from cold or fright, but rodentlike, moving rhythmically, ready to grind anything that came her way.

Alex screamed at the sight of her altered sister. But the scream emerged as a high-pitched hiss. Her back hunched uncontrollably. She was on all fours, fighting an empty ache in her belly, a hollow hunger that traveled to the synapses of her brain. There the pain was translated into a command: Chase, catch, kill!

She was a cat. And Cam was a mouse. And everything inside Alex demanded that she stalk and destroy her twin.

Fighting the urge with all her might, Alex turned toward Thantos and sank her claws into his leg. He whirled and she felt herself spin out into space, landing with a thud against a prickly hedge. Cam followed her through the air, a piece of their uncle's dark velvet robe clasped between her rodent teeth.

"Enough!" Thantos growled. "You are mere children! And ungrateful fledglings. I came to offer you help, and this is the way you greet me?!"

"Help?" Alex's voice sounded as uneven as Dylan's sometimes did. Only in her case it wasn't part child, part adult; it was feline vs. human. "You mean the way you helped Dylan?" she mewed. The effort of speaking left her throat painfully tight.

Cam's sharp little teeth were chattering. "Undo us!" she squeaked.

Thantos took a deep, calming breath, then waved his hand in their direction, mumbling again, still annoyed.

They began to morph back into their human forms. The return was more uncomfortable than the shrinking had been. Cam's limbs ached as they grew through the gray bristles of her mouse hide. Alex yowled pitifully.

"Never —" Thantos ignored their misery. "Never challenge my power!"

Despite the soreness in her jaw, Cam tried to tease her sister. "Talk about embarrassing. Do you think anyone saw us?"

"Oh, please." With a raspy tongue, Alex licked the back of her hand. "We have way more urgent issues."

"I came as a favor to your mother," Thantos was roaring as they stood before him, whole again, "and because your guardians are too busy with their own paltry affairs —"

At least Karsh let us know where Dylan is, Cam silently reminded Alex.

Mid-rant, Thantos didn't hear the aside. "This, Miranda and I have in common," he was booming, "arrogant, thankless children. Yet Miranda cares. Your mother cares deeply about your welfare. Which is why she sent me —"

Alex rolled her eyes. "Right. To turn us into pets?"

Thantos lifted his arms suddenly, as though he were going to morph them again. Through gritted teeth, he said, "Only for Miranda would I tolerate such insolence!"

"Why did you tell her that we were dead?" Cam demanded.

"Haven't you a more pressing problem?" their uncle reminded them, letting his hands fall to his sides. "Your brother is in trouble, I understand."

"You understand? Ha! You're the one who got him in trouble to begin with," Alex accused.

"Yeah," Cam added. "How did you know Dyl was in that Dumpster?"

"I didn't," Thantos said smugly. "You did. It was your

premonition, dear Camryn. I just made it available to both of you."

"Did you plant his earring in there, too?" Alex pressed.

"His earring? Oh, I see. You found something of his, did you? Excellent. To prove my good faith, I'll show you a most amusing 'trick.'"

"What are you going to do now, put us in a petting zoo?" Alex challenged.

"I'm going to show you how to perform a feat only trackers are permitted to know. How to locate someone by using an item that belonged to them, however recently or long ago. It's called the Situater."

"You're going to show us how to find Dylan?" Alex said.

Cam shuddered, thinking Als was about to blow it, about to tell Thantos that they already knew Dylan's whereabouts. *Don't,* Cam wanted to warn. *Let's suck up Uncle T's tracker trick. It'll be useful some other time.* But her sister surprised her by saying, "Ultimate cool. Guess we had you figured wrong, Uncle Thantos."

"Give me the earring." He held out his great hand.

"Nuh-uh," Cam said.

"You still don't trust me." The forceful warlock sounded exasperated, angry. "Foolish girls. Don't you know how protected you are by Miranda's devotion? Do you think I would do anything to cause her more pain? She is more to me, much more, than my brother's widow or my defiant nieces' mother. She is . . ." Thantos let it trail off. "Open your hand. Show me the Barnes boy's earring. Now!" he commanded.

Cam opened her hand, which, she was relieved to see, was still her own and not some woodland creature's. Dylan's earring lay on her palm.

"Now watch," their uncle ordered. He removed a leather pouch from his belt and took out a rough-hewn, faceted piece of rock.

But it was the pouch that fascinated Alex. She stared at it, thinking about how full of goodies it probably was and how amazing it would be to get her hands on it.

"Quartz crystal," Thantos said, holding the translucent stone over Dylan's earring. "Also known as sacred fire for its ability to trap and magnify light, to focus one's energy on a particular subject."

Light did pour onto the earring, making it gleam like a crystal ball. "Pay attention!" the warlock snapped, handing the quartz to Alex and gesturing for her to hold it over the earring.

Next he took two herbs from the sack. "Henbane," he said. "Normally one would burn this. But at this moment, I can turn it to ash in my hand. And this —" He held up a strange-looking root that seemed to have arms and legs. "Mandrake. Can you not see your brother in its form?"

Setting down the leather pouch, he didn't wait for an answer. His hands reached out and closed over both Alex's and Cam's, locking the earring, quartz, and plants together in their grasp. Then he looked up through the pine needles at the darkening sky.

The twins could feel heat rising in their palms. Thantos had told the truth when he said he could burn the henbane without a fire. Their impulse was to pull their hands away, but he held them firmly. Then, closing his eyes, their uncle recited: "*Sun and moon, earth and sky, take us deep within this sacred object's magick eye, to see what it has seen.*"

Drowsily, Cam's and Alex's eyes fluttered shut. They recognized, against the dark screen of their eyelids, the back of the mall in early light. A banged-up old red van was practically the only vehicle parked there. Leaning against it was a man smoking a cigarette. The man — about thirty, his potbelly protruding from his shiny black baseball jacket, a red knit cap down low on his head — was scanning the place. His gaze drifted past the twins — past Dylan, they realized, who must have been peering out of the Dumpster.

The man, clearly RideBoy, checked his watch, paced, waited, looked at his watch again. They could tell he was getting nervous. He threw down his cigarette and turned toward the van.

Suddenly, their view of him shifted — Dylan had obviously begun to climb out of the Dumpster. "Yo, dude, wait up!" they heard. And then the picture tumbled round and round, as Dylan's earring fell, landing on a collapsed carton next to a green plastic bag.

"Awesome," Alex breathed, opening her heavy-lidded eyes.

Cam was shaking. She tried to remove her hands from Thantos's grip, but he clamped down tighter. Alex, whose hands were mashed in the grasp, yipped, "Hey!"

"Are you so impatient with old Karsh?" their angry uncle growled. "Does he teach you but half a spell? Be still!"

"There's more?" Cam asked.

Thantos didn't answer. He looked up through the pine branches again and begrudgingly snarled: "*From this object show us how, with herbs and stones so rare, we may find young Dylan now, and see how he does fare.*"

At last, he released them. Cam and Alex opened their hands. Both the henbane and mandrake root were ash. Dylan's earring, beneath the crystal, glowed bright red. In it they could see the sandy shore, the swamp grass, the carpet of dead leaves, and Dylan! He was standing still now, holding on to a tree with one hand. His head was bent with exhaustion. He was breathing hard.

Don't give up, Alex wanted to cry out to him.

"He can't hear you, of course," Thantos said. "Do you recognize the place?"

"Sort of," Cam said.

"Look deeper. Look through the stone into the earring's gleam."

They did. The image opened out, as if they were flying backward, above Dylan. They saw the outside edge of the woods, the bay, a highway, and then the sign: SALEM 15 MILES.

CHAPTER FOURTEEN
A GRAVE SITUATION

"We're almost there." Because Miranda had asked, Ileana was taking her to a place she herself would not have chosen to go just now.

To Aron's grave, at Rock Mount Cemetery.

No archway, neither sign, nor gate indicated the entrance to the hallowed and, some said, haunted burial ground. It lay on the northern tip of Coventry, where the wind whipped most fiercely in the winter and rain fell in curtains during the spring, leaving its pathways soggy and leaf-strewn.

Thick with broad-branched trees, there was little room for the sun to break through. Darkness permeated the cemetery, even at high noon.

It was a daunting place, but Ileana had never been frightened of it, not when she was young. As a child, strong, healthy, daring — reckless, even — she had laughed at those who believed the ghost stories, dared them to come with her.

Now, for some reason, she felt just like the friends she'd laughed at.

The creaking branches overhead, the footfall-like snap of twigs in the underbrush, every noise sounded menacing, startled her, raised goose bumps. Several times she'd turned, fear spiraling up her spine, to see if they were being watched, followed.

The two women moved slowly along the rocky path, breathing hard with the effort. Miranda clutched the hem of her robe in one hand and a walking stick in the other. Ileana admitted only to herself that she, too, could have used a stick to keep her balance as they climbed.

Once, she had sprinted up this hill, light on her feet, senses sharp always. Like a young goat she had darted through the thorny bramble and branches that surrounded and protected the grave sites — and kept all of them, even the most isolated, carefully hidden.

Once, she had believed her parents were buried here and had searched for their graves, even though she knew little of her mother and nothing of her father.

Karsh, who had acted as both to her, disapproved of her trips to Rock Mount. So she'd sneak out and wander about, reading the names on the headstones, hoping, each time, to come across one that would stir something in her that would evoke some momentous feeling to let her know that here was her mother. Or father.

When none ever did, she wondered if her secret fantasy wasn't reality. That somehow her true parents were alive, that they were, in fact, Aron and Miranda DuBaer. Though they were hardly old enough, they were good, and kind, and strong, and loving. And she resembled them. Her metallic-gray eyes were exactly the same as theirs. She imagined that living with Karsh was some kind of test. And if she passed it, Aron and Miranda would come to claim her, to welcome her back into her true home.

Ileana had held that fantasy close for many years. She didn't give it up entirely until she was fourteen — and learned that Miranda was pregnant and would soon start a real family. It was irrational, she knew, to feel betrayed. But she had.

As if Miranda intuited the teen witch's envy, she'd spent more time with her, listening, teaching, nurturing. Acting much like the mother Ileana had always wanted.

And then the twins came, and Miranda vanished.

* * *

With increasing difficulty, the fragile women traipsed up the steep incline. Ileana stole a glance at Miranda, wondering whether Aron's widow — who had gently but firmly insisted on this trek — was really up to it.

Finally, they came to the crest of the hill where Aron had been buried amid many, many generations of DuBaers.

It was hard to find his modest stone because here, taller than the traditional prickly hedges, were flowers! A garden of fragrant flowering herbs ringed the DuBaer family plot.

Who had done this? Who had so lovingly and diligently kept it up?

Karsh, thought Ileana.

Thantos, thought Miranda.

It had been many years since the young widow had cried and keened for her husband. Not since that terrible moment when Karsh had told her of Aron's death, had brought her his bloody cloak, and she had gone mad.

Had her years at Rolling Hills rendered her numb? Or had she been there because her feelings were too deeply buried?

Miranda dropped to her knees amid the rosemary and thyme, the stalks of lavender and pink and blue blossoming sage, the towering sunflowers and creeping phlox.

She leaned against the small marker that bore her beloved's name, feeling the smooth marble against her forehead and the rush of tears against her cheek. Her shoulders heaved as she wept, sobbed, shook in a churning gale of sorrow.

To give Miranda privacy, Ileana turned away.

In that moment, she was swept by a wave of fear. Something rustled in the bramble beyond the flowers. Something untamed — hyenas, coyotes, wild dogs — gurgled soft, snickering sounds. She whirled toward Miranda, to see if she'd heard anything. But the grieving woman was lost in her own world.

With a shush, the noise in the bushes faded. The only sounds Ileana heard were Miranda's wrenching sobs — and her own heart, breaking for the woman. Quietly, Ileana walked over and stroked Miranda's thick, silky hair.

"I used to wish you were my mother," she murmured, lowering herself to the wet ground, to sit next to Miranda as her weeping subsided.

"I know," Miranda whispered.

"I never knew much about her," the young witch continued, "only that her name was Beatrice, and she had blond hair —"

"And sparkling brown eyes, and cheeks always rosy

with brewing mischief. She was quick-witted, your mother, and regal in her bearing if not her heritage." Miranda turned from the grave and peered at Ileana through tear-swollen eyes.

"You knew her?" Ileana pulled back, surprised. Why hadn't she known that?

"And of course, your father, too," Miranda affirmed.

Ileana's face turned cold. "Father? Don't speak of it! If it's Lord Thantos you mean, I still don't believe it — and if it is true, I can't bear it."

Miranda shook her head. "I understand, but you . . . you don't know him —"

"And whose fault is that?!" Ileana leaped up, her face contorted in anger. "Perhaps it's you who don't know him. He killed your husband! He's an uncaring, greedy monster, a murderous predator, scornful of anyone who gets in his way."

With effort, Miranda rose and grasped Ileana's shoulders. "I could never believe that Thantos was a murderer. What possible reason would he have to cut down his own brother? They were bound not only by blood but by family loyalty. They ran a business together, one that has, as Aron intended, benefited millions of people."

Ileana glowered. "Thantos wanted Aron dead and pushed Fredo to do it."

Miranda shook her head wearily. "No, child. Poor Fredo was never . . . right, never bright as the others. He's always been dull and easily influenced."

Ileana whirled. Again, she heard it. Something in the bramble, this time a creature that huffed and grumbled rather than laughed.

She caught an overbearing sweet, oily scent — more like a noxious cosmetic than an herb. Once more there was a rustling in the bushes, though there was no breeze. She looked up at the trees to see if any were swaying. They were still. She cocked her ear. If only her senses were keen again. If only she could hear and see and smell as she had before the trial, before discovering that Thantos DuBaer had fathered her. Then, if someone — even a spirit — were nearby, she would know.

"He was born afflicted, the child of Leila's old age," Miranda was saying. "All Aron and Thantos ever did was to try and help him."

Gently, Miranda turned Ileana's chin, forcing the edgy young witch to look at her. "You hate Thantos for one reason only — though you don't know why he behaved as he did."

Ileana couldn't stop the torrent of angry tears. "He threw me away! His own daughter. Never to recognize me, never to nurture, to teach . . ." The words *never to*

love would not come out. "What kind of monster does that?"

Now Miranda stroked Ileana's hair, which was as tangled as threads of Florentine gold. "What kind of monster? The kind that had been hurt so deeply that he couldn't even look into the tiny, angry red face of his newborn child. Remember, dear child, he had just lost Beatrice —"

"Yes! Because of me," Ileana ranted. "Is that what you're saying? That she died giving birth to me, so he hated me, wanted to bury me with my mother?" She had said what she hadn't even known she'd been thinking.

"Never!" Miranda gasped.

"No excuse!" Ileana spun away from her. "She wasn't the first to die in childbirth. Other fathers cherish their babies, the one living reminder —"

"Exactly. You were all that Thantos, bent and broken, could not be reminded of. Dear Ileana, has no one ever told you the full story?"

Ileana clenched her teeth. "Story, or fantasy? Made up by him to deceive you."

"No, he did not make it up," Miranda said evenly. "Remember, I was there. I was Aron's beloved, his brother's bride. I bore witness to it all."

Stubbornly skeptical, Ileana shook her head. But she remained silent as Miranda led her to a bench near the imposing crypt of Ephram DuBaer, the first of the illustrious family to come to the New World, to the Plymouth Colony, where his skills as a botanist and healer brought him wealth and renown.

The carved bench on which they sat felt cold to Ileana, as cold and unwelcoming as her so-called father. But Miranda took her hand and stroked it gently as she passed along all that she knew.

Soon after Aron and Miranda were betrothed, the twins' mother said, Thantos fell in love, too.

Her name was Beatrice, Ileana's mother, Beatrice Hazlett. She was beautiful, bright, and strong-willed, which Miranda and Aron had agreed was just the sort of mate the self-centered, stubborn Thantos needed.

All the family were thrilled for him — except for Leila, his mother. Perhaps she saw too much of herself in Beatrice, viewed the headstrong young beauty as a threat to her own dominating nature. But Leila claimed that it was because Beatrice was lowborn, of an undistinguished lineage.

The Hazletts, Leila was convinced, were poets and dreamers and had produced no great witches or warlocks. Miranda shook her head in wonder. "This despite the fact that they were distant relatives of the Antayus clan, our dear Karsh's people."

Aron had argued with his mother; Miranda had,

too — as much as she dared. "Leila was a formidable creature," Miranda said.

Ileana nodded knowingly. Though she had met Leila only as a spirit, "formidable," even "fearsome," did not begin to describe her grandmother's aura.

Leila vowed she would never accept Beatrice as a daughter. She pressured Thantos not to marry her, did everything she could think of to discredit Ileana's mother and stop the nuptials. Miranda recalled how Leila had constantly harped on Beatrice's background, how she'd reminded Thantos that he was acting in haste and that his judgment was flawed because he was on the rebound, not in his true mind.

Marrying anyone at that vulnerable time, let alone a Hazlett, would only be done out of spite, Leila had believed, and could only end in disaster.

Only one of Leila's sons was as obstinate and assertive as she — and that was Thantos. Of course, he went against his mother's will. And of course, Leila refused to attend the wedding. She warned Thantos that should he and Beatrice become parents, she would never set eyes upon their child. The powerful and mighty Leila DuBaer would have nothing to do with the baby.

Ileana gasped. Leila's spirit had begged her forgiveness. Now she knew why.

Thantos insisted they be married at once, Miranda's

tale continued, a year before Aron and she were to wed. When Beatrice died in childbirth, Leila rushed to "comfort" her eldest. But she also assured Thantos that Ileana's mother's death was the result of his pigheadedness and of Beatrice's ancestral weakness.

In his bereaved state, Thantos chose to believe her.

He also believed that Leila was demanding he make a choice — Miranda thought that in her cunning way, Leila was — a choice between his mother and his daughter, an infant whose blood might carry Beatrice's defiance. If Leila would have nothing to do with Ileana, neither then would Thantos.

"So he asked Karsh, one of the great warlocks of his day and your grandfather Nathaniel's best friend, to look after you. And to hide his pain," Miranda supposed, "Thantos buried himself in work."

He did whatever he could to forget his marriage and his child — and lived to show his mother that he was just as capable of bringing glory to the DuBaers as Aron, who he'd always thought she loved better.

"The truth is, Ileana, he could not bear to see you. You reminded him of . . . everything he wanted to forget."

It was too much, too much to take in all at once. When Miranda said nothing more, Ileana filled the uncomfortable silence. "Then my mother's grave isn't here among the DuBaers, is it?"

Miranda shook her head. "It's on the other side of the island, in a far fairer and gentler place. The cemetery, in fact, where Karsh's ancestors rest. I will take you there one day."

Ileana suddenly remembered something. "You said that Thantos was on the rebound? From whom?"

Miranda shrugged. "His one true love, he once said. We never found out. But this you must know, Ileana. I believe Thantos was mistaken, misguided in his treatment of you, yet he is a decent man."

"He's scum," Ileana quarreled.

"I would trust him with Apolla's and Artemis's lives," Miranda insisted.

Ileana whirled on her, infuriated, affronted. "You mean Camryn's and Alexandra's lives? What would you know of them? Your wisdom, like your power, is truly diminished. A real mother would have known they were alive. You weren't here. . . ." She caught herself and, instantly, she was ashamed.

Miranda felt sick, weak, stabbed, but she couldn't let Ileana see it. That would have hurt the wounded young witch even more. She simply said, "I got a message from . . . from Camryn and Alexandra. They needed help —"

"What? What's wrong?" Ileana began to tremble. The twins had needed her, and she hadn't even heard them. But Miranda, who she'd just accused of being an unfit mother, had? That was how badly broken she was, Ileana realized with dread.

"Their brother —"

"Dylan?"

"Yes," Miranda said. "He's disappeared, and they fear the worst."

"Has Karsh gone to them?"

Miranda looked surprised. "No. I didn't get the impression he was overly concerned. Anyway, I didn't contact him. This is a chance for their uncle to prove his goodness. My girls needed help. I sent Thantos to them."

Furious, frightened, Ileana turned so abruptly, she felt light-headed. "We've got to go."

Miranda was puzzled. "Now? Why?"

Ileana grasped her arm. "I have an appointment and I'm not leaving you here. End of story." With that, she rushed her aunt out of the herb garden and hurried her down the steep path.

Perhaps if Miranda had not been so surprised and Ileana not so panicked, one of them might have heard the commotion they'd left behind. Two creatures, struggling to break free of the clinging brambles and sticky vines encasing them, tumbled out of the bushes, with thorns poking out of their flesh and clothing at every angle.

"Tsuris, you let her escape!" the short, fat cactus whined.

"Me? I told you it was bad luck to hide in a cemetery!" the taller, spiny critter shrieked.

"At least we found her!"

"Past tense, Vey, you slacker! Let's go. Sooner or later, she's bound to go back to the old man's shack."

CHAPTER FIFTEEN
SALEM WOODS

"I don't get it," Jason said again. "Are you sure you don't want me to drive you all the way into town?"

"No," Cam answered, staring out the window, searching the roadside. "I'm trying to toughen Alex up for soccer this year."

"And you're going to start her off with a fifteen-mile hike? Condolences," the tall, dark, and studly boy called back to Alex, who was scanning the other side of the highway. "You have my sympathy. Personally, I think your sister's crazy."

"Runs in the family," Alex answered.

"Alex!" Cam snapped. "That is so unfunny!"

Alex shrugged, a little startled herself at what she'd

blurted — even if it was true. A sudden chill drove Miranda from her mind. "I think we're there."

"Me, too," Cam said, twisting the patchwork quilt in her lap and sounding a lot less superior than she had a second before.

"This is it?" Jason slowed reluctantly and pulled over to the side of the road. "It's going to be dark out soon. Why would you want to do this now?"

They'd run into the concerned hottie about a minute after their psycho uncle split — saying he'd done for them what he could and had to get back to their mother now. Miranda needed him, Thantos had suddenly decided. She shouldn't be left alone.

"I mean, come on —" Jason surveyed the thickly forested area around them and shook his head. "With Dylan missing and all . . ."

"That's just why we're doing this," Alex announced. Cam spun around to glare at her. "You know," she said pointedly to her distrustful twin, "to work off some nervous energy."

Nervous energy became icy trembling as they trudged through the swampy woods. Cam wrapped Miranda's shawl around her neck like a scarf. Alex hiked up the collar of her camouflage jacket. Neither of them spoke for a while.

Eyes wide, senses honed, they moved slowly in

what they hoped was the direction of the bay, looking for the sandy landscape Cam had described — and that they'd both seen through Thantos's crystal.

Alex's nostrils were filling with the scent of salt and brine. And something else, too. A jumble of odors that had nothing to do with this time and place. A fragrance at once stale and seductive that reminded her of the spirit she and Cam had once conjured, the awesome specter of Leila DuBaer, their grandmother.

"Leila plus," Cam whispered, grabbing Alex's hand. "Don't you get the feeling we're not alone here? And I don't mean just rabbits, squirrel, deer, and Dylan, either."

"Although he's in the mix," Alex confirmed. "I smell him, but faintly."

"Faintly is so not Dyl's odor." Cam laughed tensely. "Not in that laundry hamper he calls home."

"Uh, did you hear that?" Alex squeezed her sister's fingers.

"Nuh — no," Cam stammered. "But something . . . icky . . . just brushed against my shoulder, Als."

"Like a cobweb?" Alex breathed in again. "Or a musty old robe or something?"

"Old? How 'bout Jurassic? Talk about cold feet," Cam said, feeling brackish water squishing in her shoes.

"What's that poem? 'The woods are lovely, dark, and

deep, but I have promises to keep —' You know, by Robert Frost."

"This can't have been the woods he was talking about," Cam ventured. "But I wouldn't be surprised if he were here."

"Who, Robert Frost? He's dead."

"Duh," Cam said.

They slogged along, staring, sniffing, holding hands. "Bad thought," Cam broke the silence. "What if this is a setup? What if Thantos led us here —"

"For what?"

Cam shrugged, then shrieked. "Something just . . . REACHED OUT AND TOUCHED ME!"

"Ah, the woods are full of telephone commercials," Alex tried to joke, then said seriously, "I smelled it, Cam. It's . . . a person. People. You know, like Leila. Old . . . people."

"You mean dead people." Cam cut to the chase.

"Well . . . yeah. Spirits, ghosts, whatever. I think we're . . . like, someplace we're not supposed to be."

"Understatement alert," Cam said. "But we can't just evacuate the premises. Dylan's here, too, right? You smelled him. I feel his presence."

An unexpected gust of warm air ruffled Alex's hair and wafted against Cam's cheek. *Go back, I pray you,* a deep, wounded voice urged.

Alex ran her fingers over her head. The breeze had left her scalp tingling. "Did you hear that?" she whispered to Cam. "A woman's voice. Young, sad . . ."

"No." Cam was stroking her cheek, where a feeling of comforting warmth still lingered.

"Saddest voice I ever heard," Alex murmured. "What is this place?"

"A graveyard," Cam answered, certain, but mystified about how she knew.

Alex nodded. "It's a witches' graveyard. A . . . some kind of burial ground."

They were almost at the water's edge. The sounds of the bay came to them, waves lapping against a shore, seabirds cawing. "Look! There's the tree," Cam said excitedly. "The one Dylan was leaning against —"

If you love him, go back, the voice warned again.

Alex spun around. "Where are you? Who are you?" she asked, peering into the graying light.

There was no one there, no answer.

And then they saw Dylan! He was collapsed on the ground at the foot of the big tree. His eyes were closed. In his hands he clutched the predator's cap.

For the sake of him who loves you, go now, the heartbroken voice whispered. *Do not lead him this way.*

"Alex!" Cam's shout brought her back to reality. Her

sister was kneeling in the gritty mud beside Dylan, hugging him. "Hurry. He's breathing! He's okay, I think."

"Dylan!" Alex shouted, elated, rushing to them. Up close she could see that mixed in the dirt and mud smeared across Dyl's face was a dried reddish-brown crust of blood. "He's cut. That creep must have hit him —"

Cam found a plastic container half buried in the sand. She rinsed and filled it with fresh seawater and hurried back to Dylan. As they washed his face, he stirred, came back to consciousness.

"I'm sorry," was the first thing he said when he recognized them. "It was whack. I shouldn't have gone alone —"

"Hey, no probs," Alex assured him. "We found you. You're okay. Or you will be as soon as we —"

"I'll be okay, but his next victim won't." Dylan tried to get up but couldn't manage it. "He's going after someone else. I heard him when I was in the back of his van. I heard him setting up another 'date.' Same lies. Telling her he's sixteen and into parasailing and white-water rafting and hot-dog skiing. For all I know, he's got her already."

The outburst exhausted him. He slumped back heavily against the tree.

"Is that his hat?" Alex asked as Dylan's eyes drifted

shut. "Kenya described it," she explained. Glancing at Cam, she added silently, *We can track the bozo through his cap — thanks to Uncle T.*

Yeah, if we had quartz crystal and mandrake and chickenbrain —

Henbane, Alex corrected her. *Voilà!* She tossed something to Camryn.

Unc the skunk's herb pouch! Cam was impressed. *How did you — ?*

I'm getting soooo good, her sister crowed. *I did the beg-and-boost thing; you know, stared at it, wanted it, wished for it — and boom!*

Gently, Alex took RideBoy's knit cap from Dylan.

"He shoved me out of the van," the boy murmured. "I snagged his hat when he pushed me. And I've got his license plate number. How's Kenya doing?"

"Better than Mom and Dad," Cam said.

"Oh, man." Dylan held his head in his hands. "I really messed up this time."

"Well, yeah."

"But you also caught a creep," Alex pointed out, brushing mud and leaves from Dylan's hair. "I mean, with his license plate number and your description of him and Kenya's story of what went down — and don't forget his hat. That may turn out to be really valuable," she said, glancing significantly at Cam. *If we can grab a couple of*

minutes' worth of privacy to play Unc's tracker trick with it. "I mean, a really valuable . . . you know, piece of evidence."

Cam nodded. "Know what, Dyl? My cellular won't work down here. Why don't Alex and I try to find better reception, while you just hang here for a few minutes more, okay?"

"Sure," Dylan said groggily.

"Okay. Be back in a minute," she assured him as they started away.

"How come both of you have to go?" Dyl called after them.

They stopped, looked searchingly at each other, and turned back to Dylan. His eyes were shut; his breathing was heavy but rhythmic. "He's out," Alex whispered. "Come on. We'll do the Situater, find out where the sicko's skulking, and be right back."

They went toward the choppy bay, then followed the uneven shoreline to an unexpected opening in the sea grass. Walking inland, between the rustling reeds, they came to an alley of overhanging branches. At the end of it, several yards of brush and trees had been cleared. The tamped-down area formed a nearly perfect circle surrounded by stones and strangely imposing evergreens, majestic and menacing.

An icy wind rattled through the trees, raising goose

bumps on Cam's neck and arms. Alex felt it, too, as she stared up at the towering firs and spruces. "Maybe this isn't the right spot," she ventured. "There's something . . . I don't know . . . ugly about it, don't you think?"

"It's majorly spooky," Cam concurred. "There's something here that . . . I can't explain it, Als, but it reminds me of or makes me think of Karsh. Not *our* Karsh, not our funny, scary-looking, nubby-headed, sweet grand-guardian, but a cold, gray, lost Karsh —"

Alex shuddered and, in a gesture of defiance, pulled open Thantos's leather pouch. "Let's do this thing," she said. "Now. Situate RideBoy, 911 the cops, and get out of here. Fast."

CHAPTER SIXTEEN
CHOICES

Ileana was angry. She was an equal-opportunity blamer.

Enraged at Thantos, she stomped around her cottage, ticking off the reasons. She blamed him for tricking Miranda. The greedy, power-hungry warlock had pretended to be taking care of her, when he was really taking advantage of her mental state. Miranda had blocked out her own memories. Thantos came sweeping in with his version of what had happened that November morning fifteen years ago — fiction to further his self-centered agenda.

Ileana blamed him for trying to lure Camryn and Alexandra away from their duty to serve humanity to his desire to have them serve him. With the power of Aron's family on his side, he'd truly be omnipotent. Woe to those who would cross him. Should the twins prove too smart to fall under his spell? He'd kill them.

Mostly, she blamed Thantos for what happened the day of her own birth. He'd rejected her and, from that day forward, treated her as nothing more than an ordinary, irritating stranger. That she could occasionally be irritating, Ileana would be the first to admit, but never was she or would she be ordinary!

Ileana blamed Miranda, too. How could such a once insightful and powerful witch be so easily ensnared? This was not the Miranda of her memory, far from the kindhearted, brilliant shining star Ileana had worshiped — and wanted to be.

How could this once exquisite and powerful woman have deteriorated so much? What kind of mentor was she now? What kind of parent could she be — sending a dangerous, deranged tracker to "protect" her children?

A parent with neither experience nor good instincts to guide her, Ileana concluded, a role model for dismal failure.

Ileana's harshest fury was reserved for herself. How could her powers fail her now? How could she have fallen so far into the pity pot that she couldn't climb out to help the twins, her charges. Her cousins!

She threw off her heavy cape and smoothed the seams of the gauzy midnight-blue gown she wore beneath it. The choice to run off to Marble Bay in her current condition was not wise. What help could she be in this strange, weakened state?

Yet what choice did she have? Miranda had sent Thantos to them — Lord Bad Dad himself, everybody's favorite in the I'd Rather Be Cloned Than Have Him for a Father Sweepstakes. That kind of help was a disaster waiting to happen.

Ileana shuddered suddenly. What if she ended up like Miranda; what would it be like to spend more than a decade powerless? No! She stomped her stiletto-heeled foot. That would never happen to her. She would not allow it. She would regain her gifts by sheer willpower. If anyone could will her magick back, she could!

Briefly, Ileana considered asking Karsh to come with her, but thought better of it.

He would try to prevent her from going, perform a spell to keep her grounded, and try even harder to talk her into letting him go in her stead. Which would make her, for all Coventry to see, the pitiable weakling she had become.

No way! She might have lost her powers, but not her pride.

Problem — immediate rather than long range — she had no way to quickly get to Marble Bay. She was already the flightless bird Karsh might have tried to turn her into. She could not rely on glorious wings to carry her soaring to the coastal Massachusetts town. Any other means of transportation would take too long.

So Ileana did something she had sneered at others for doing. She admitted she needed help — and, swallowing that cherished pride, she summoned Brice Stanley.

The handsome warlock she had almost given her heart to had betrayed her. Since the trial, where he'd testified on behalf of Thantos, she had cast him out of her life. But the willful witch was desperate. And the warlock movie star owned a private jet.

Brice was the fastest route to the twins. And, as she knew he would be, *People*'s pick for Hollywood hottie of the year was eager to send his plane. No doubt believing, Ileana supposed, that the gesture was the fastest route back into her good graces.

He'd be wrong about that.

Ileana did not forgive easily. But the heinous loss of her powers had an upside. It had made her desperately practical. And at the moment, there was no faster, easier way to get to Cam and Alex.

Karsh was alarmed.

He was anxious about the twins. He was needed in a place he could not be. He had tried to help them telepathically. He'd "forwarded" his vision of Dylan's whereabouts to Camryn. He'd telegraphed the longitude and latitude to Alexandra. He believed absolutely in the daughters of Aron and Miranda. They would save the boy's life. He would not have to go there.

And yet. He was nervous. What if something went wrong, something the not-yet-initiated pair could not handle?

Karsh stared out the window of his cottage. Ileana's cat, Boris, was wandering alone in the woods. Suddenly, he knew: His impetuous, willful charge had gone to the twins, was already on her way.

His anxiety quotient was upped to all-out alarm. What made her think she was a match for Thantos? Her hatred would blind her; her diminished state would impair her; her pride would be her downfall. Here was a tragedy in the making. Unless he was there to prevent it.

But he could not be. His every rational thought, every cell in his body warned against it. Besides, he was needed here, to relay the truth, to open the door to the twins' future. He could not risk leaving Coventry Island right now — especially not to venture into the woods of Salem.

Yet how could he not? If the twins were Ileana's responsibility, the powerless but still impetuous witch was his. What choice did that leave him? If he didn't intervene and the worst happened . . .

He could not even think about that now. He needed every ounce of intellect and positive energy to forge his decision.

Seconds passed that felt like hours. With a heavy heart, Karsh knew what had to be done. In the basement of his cottage was a very old wooden trunk. He'd never opened it before but he knew its contents. Most would be sorted through later, by others. What he needed right now lay on the very bottom. Gold-threaded, beaded with sparkling gems, it was a handsome cloak.

He'd never worn it before, of course, never believed he would put it on by himself, alive and willingly. Nevertheless, after dusting off his best waistcoat and vest, Karsh donned the awesome cape.

One other thing the aged warlock had to do before he left. The notebook in which he'd painstakingly recorded all that Ileana and the twins needed to know had been hastily stuffed into a random book the day Miranda surprised him by showing up at his door.

Just before he left to follow the irrepressible child he'd raised as his own, Karsh retrieved it and inserted it instead into the most appropriate tome he could find: *Forgiveness or Vengeance: Righting Ancient Wrongs.* He pressed the worn book to his lips before returning it to the shelf.

Their father was ruthless, faithless, and violent — a warlock from the wealthiest clan on Coventry Island. Their mother was simpler — ambitious, greedy, treacherous, she was a descendent of notorious crooks and con men. But because she was not a witch, Tsuris and Vey were only half warlock. They possessed a bit of the wit of each of their parents. Hence, they were also half-wits.

Because they'd grown up with their mother on the mainland — in a little beach cottage in the gated community of Malibu — and not on the island where they might have been trained, they were ignorant of the craft. Ignoramuses, some said, which sounded to them very classically Greek.

What Tsuris and Vey had learned, however, was this: A huge inheritance had once awaited them. But now, with their father incarcerated, their share of the money, their mother had told them, was threatened.

It was all the fault of that vile, vain creature who had been chasing after Brice Stanley, the movie star their mama most adored. If that weren't enough, Ms. Ileana DuBaer was their uncle Thantos's child. She therefore stood to snag the loot she'd so cleverly denied them by putting their daddy in jail.

They must make her pay for it, their mother had decreed.

They had missed their chance at Rock Mount Cemetery. They believed she would next show at Karsh's cottage. So there they went, hid, and waited.

Because they had not even the basic warlock skills, let alone the more advanced like mind reading, they had no idea what Karsh was up to or where the old man was going as he put on his very gaudy traveling cloak.

They decided to follow him anyway.

CHAPTER SEVENTEEN
THE HAT TRICK

They were inside a narrow room, a space capsule with cheap black velvet and faux leopard skin stapled to the walls and an orange shag carpet on the floor. The fabric was ripped in spots and rusty metal showed through.

It wasn't until they saw Dylan collapsed in a corner that Cam and Alex realized that they were looking at the interior of RideBoy's van, which he'd apparently done up like some kind of den.

Dylan was curled up on his side. His cheek was bruised, puffy, scraped. They were looking down at him.

"Wise guy, right?" they heard. "What are you, a junior G-man or something?"

"Junior G-man? What are you, Dick Tracy?" Dylan sneered, rolling onto his back.

A hand lashed out and struck his injured cheek. Droplets of blood formed at the cut. Dylan, his hands bound with clothesline rope, tried to scramble to his feet. The hand shot out again, pushing him back down.

"He's tied up," Cam whispered, appalled.

"Hold the crystal steady," Alex commanded, wrinkling her nose. Her hands stunk of burned mandrake root and henbane. She didn't like standing there, shivering, in the eerie, swamp-stinking circle of rocks. But the spell Thantos had taught them was working.

She and Cam were seeing Dylan from his kidnapper's point of view — more specifically, from the point of view of the slimebag's hat.

"He's getting back into the driver's seat," Cam said. "Als! Isn't that the road we just drove over? He's heading toward Salem —"

"Duh. Where he's going to dump Dylan in the woods," Alex reminded her. "And the credits are going to roll on this part of the movie —"

She opened her eyes, stretched, and blinked at the fading daylight, while Cam kept hers shut, clinging to the crystal and the cap.

It had been like watching a miniseries. Following

Dylan's earring had been part one. Today's episode filled in what had happened after the earring fell out.

The potbellied guy had looked up (startled at Dylan's "Yo, dude, wait up!" Alex assumed). From the point of view of the grungy knit cap, they saw Dylan walking slowly toward the man.

"What do you want?" the guy had called to him. "Hey, what are you doing, taking down my license number? What's up with you, kid?"

Dylan had turned abruptly and pulled out a cell phone — which Kenya might have lent him, or it could have been Robbie Meeks's, Cam thought. Anyway, he had a cell phone for about a minute . . . just until the blubbery bozo ran after him, knocked the phone out of his hand, and dragged him, in a headlock, back to the rusty red van.

Dyl struggled. He got in a solid punch, a kick or two, and had almost wriggled out of the headlock, when the perv picked up a piece of pipe and put out Dylan's lights with a blow to the side of his head.

"What a sleaze," Alex had hollered, outraged, as the man threw Dylan into the back of his van and pulled shut the sliding door.

"Whoops. There it is," Cam said, still staring through the quartz crystal. "The pig's trying to shove Dyl out of the van. Dylan's trying to grab the guy's head with his hands tied. Alex, look. He got his hat instead. And . . . there goes my bro, hat's-eye view, sailing out of the van, rolling over and over down a hill, bouncing in ditches and against trees. Ugh! No wonder Dylan looked so beat up when we found him."

She straightened up, a little green at the gills. "That was majorly disgusting."

"Hang on," Alex said, keeping Cam's hands clamped around the hat. "Don't forget the rest. We've got to find RideBoy before he hooks up with some other gullible girl —"

"Do you remember how it goes?" Cam asked. "It's like: *From this crummy dumby's cap show us how —*"

"Maybe we'd better stick with the original words," Alex suggested.

"Fine." Cam rolled her eyes. "*From this* object *show us how, with herbs and stones so rare —*"

"*We may find RideBoy now,*" Alex recited, "*and see how he does fare.*"

Their eyelids grew instantly heavy and fluttered shut. Their hearts jumped into their throats as they were hurled backward, up over the van, above the highway, farther and farther into space until they could see the rusty blood-colored truck making its way toward the narrow streets of Salem town center.

They saw the van leisurely cruising along a cobble-stone avenue near the historically restored wharf. Three times RideBoy circled the area, each time driving more slowly.

The pier was dotted with strolling tourists. A young girl was sitting on an outdoor table at one of the food stalls. She was surveying the sparse crowd, craning her neck, looking this way and that. The girl was obviously searching for someone, waiting for something —

"She's it," Alex cried. "She's his next victim. We've got to find a way to warn her!"

"Als, look! There's a police car parked in front of that gift shop," Cam shouted.

"That's probably why the predator hasn't stopped."

"I can phone them," Cam said. "I mean, I can phone 911 and explain what's shaking —"

"Can you read the numbers on the cop cruiser?" Alex asked, eyes still shut, hands holding on to Cam's. "Then you can tell 911 there's already a patrol car on the scene."

"Okay," Cam said after a moment. "I've got it." Pulling away from her sister, she flipped open her cell phone and punched in the police emergency digits.

With a grunt of disgust, Alex threw down the knit cap and walked toward the water. Her intention was to clean the herbal ashes from her hands. She wished she could as easily wash away the ugly scenes Thantos's trick had revealed.

Suddenly, everything was freaking her — her dirty hands, the feeling that the forest was full of spirits, the voices she'd heard in the woods, the weird circle of rocks she'd stumbled upon in the middle of nowhere, the thick soggy leaves and wet sand underfoot, the quickly descending darkness, even the sound of wind whistling across the water. And then there was Cam's feeling or premonition or vision of Karsh as a cold, gray, changed being.

About the only consolation, Alex thought, elbowing roughly through the rattling cattails, was the pale face of the full moon overhead.

But where was Karsh? Where was Ileana? Did Miranda's appearance have anything to do with their disappearances?

Alex shuddered. In spite of the chill night air, she felt a rush of hot rage.

No biggie, she told herself as her hypersensitive ears caught the slam of a car door from the road above.

Anger was her element. And what had just happened was an old familiar flipperoo, an emotion exchange. She'd morphed upset into anger. Annoyance, resentment, irritation, Alex would take them over sadness, self-pity, and disappointment any day of the week.

And speaking of exchanges, she mused miserably, had their guardians okayed one without bothering to check it out with them? Had Karsh and Ileana made some whack deal since their mother was back in the picture that Miranda and Uncle T would take Karsh's and Ileana's places?

"Help!!!"

Alex spun around.

In the bright moonlight, a blonde wrapped in a cocoon of cobalt-blue silk was rolling wretchedly down the hill. The tumbling creature landed against the fern-cushioned base of a tree. "Is on the way!" she finished.

"Ileana?!" Alex called.

"Is it really you?" Cam rushed toward the fallen woman. "Yes! How excellent. I knew you'd come."

"Help me up!" the imperious witch demanded, extending her hand.

Alex ran back through the reeds to the rock circle. Together, she and Cam heaved Ileana to her stiletto-sandaled feet.

Their guardian was a mess. One of her heels was broken. Her golden hair, plastered with leaves, looked greasy and unkempt. Her naturally pale face was sallow and gaunt, made more startling by the dark rings around her once-lively gray eyes. And her robe, torn from her fall, was caked in grime.

"All right, then." Ileana dusted off what she could. "Fill me in. What's the problem?"

Alex and Cam looked at each other, confused. Normally — though that was hardly a word they associated with their quick-witted guardian — Ileana would not have had to ask. Especially since they'd been pretty precise about their predicament when they'd sent for her.

"Well, it was about Dylan," Cam said.

"But we've found him. And we've also situat — I mean, *located*," Alex quickly corrected herself, not wanting to tip the volatile witch to the fact that they knew the forbidden Situater spell. "We located this evil creep who's been stalking girls on the Internet."

"I just called the police and told them where to find him," Cam added.

"And you did this . . . all by yourselves?" Ileana asked.

Uh-oh, Alex thought, she'd blown it. Ileana had read her mind and now knew they'd been performing tracker magick, unauthorized spells. Flinching, she waited for their guardian to explode.

Cam must have come to the same conclusion, because she took her sister's hand and they both stood looking up at Ileana as if she were wearing judge's robes and not one good shoe and a ratty, wrinkled gown.

The explosion came. But it was an eruption so weird that it rendered Alex and Cam speechless. Instead of raging at them, Ileana wept.

The distraught, disheveled witch swayed before them, her face hidden in her hands, her thin shoulders wracked with sobs.

They didn't know what to do. Their instincts were muddled by shock. To comfort their independent guardian might infuriate her, but to witness her meltdown without doing or saying anything seemed cruel.

"Don't look at me," Ileana cried. "I'm so ashamed."

The baffled twins responded at the same time: "Ashamed? Get out —" Alex blurted; "No, no, it's okay," Cam crooned reassuringly.

Ileana limped over to one of the large rocks surrounding the circle and sat down. "I'm useless," she wailed, "and what's worse, I'm *unnecessary*! You didn't need me at all. You handled everything without my help. Thantos was here, wasn't he?"

She leaped to her feet and struck a more familiar Ileana pose — eyes flashing, hands on her hips. "And he helped you, didn't he?"

Without thinking, Cam nodded.

"At what price?" Ileana demanded. "Are you going over to the dark side now or after your initiation? Oh, don't tell me," she snarled sarcastically. "He blabbed, right? Gave you all the Coventry skinny? Dished the dirt, did he? He didn't happen to mention that *he's my father*?!"

"Well, actually —" Cam began.

"We —" Alex started.

"Or did you already know that?" Ileana cut them off. "As, it seems, everybody did but me! Talk about the dark side, I've been in the dark for years! Well, don't worry. You won't have to put up with me much longer. I'm thinking of leaving Coventry."

CHAPTER EIGHTEEN
INTRUDERS IN THE CIRCLE

"I knew it, I knew it!" Alex ranted, startling Cam as well as Ileana. "You made a deal, didn't you? You and Karsh. You're dropping us. You're turning us over to . . . to a mother who's a total stranger to us and can't even do the Transporter spell on her own and . . . and a father — *yours!* — who is probably the coldest warlock on the planet!"

It was the shaken witch's turn to be speechless. Biting her lip, Ileana turned her head abruptly. Though her classically carved nose and obstinate chin were thrust in the air, her gray eyes seemed ready to gush again.

"Is that true?" Cam gasped. "Are we being . . . dumped?"

"Well, tell her," Alex demanded. "Are you *bored* with us? Are we cutting into your precious *schmooze* time with Hollywood hotties? And what's the story on Karsh?"

"He'd never leave us," Cam interjected nervously. "I mean, Als, he's been with us forever. And we didn't do anything to upset him. Did we?" she asked Ileana.

"Of course not!" a rasping voice responded cheerfully. Parting the low hanging branches of a soaring evergreen, stepping carefully over the border stones, Karsh entered the circle.

Cam and Alex's delight was multiplied by awe at the sight of the old warlock.

He looked magnificent!

Their guardian's guardian was decked out as they'd never seen him. Over his familiar black velvet trousers, vest, and waistcoat, he wore a thin cloak. Embroidered in gold threads, interwoven with sparkling gems, it shimmered in the moonlight, floating like wings behind him. From a scarlet ribbon, his Exalted Elder's medallion glinted on his chest like a warrior's campaign decoration.

Most stunning of all, Karsh's face, which was usually covered with the ghostly white powder he wore to preserve his aged skin — and to rivet the attention of fidgety fledglings — was bare and warmly brown. Even his nappy white hair looked neatly trimmed.

So Cam and Alex were totally bewildered when, upon seeing this elegant, "new" Karsh, Ileana fell to her knees before him and began to cry again. "Oh, no. Please no," she sobbed. "It can't be time."

To their further amazement, Karsh did nothing to comfort her, but lay a wizened hand on her head.

"So you found your brother?" he said to the twins, all smiles and kindness. "I'm very proud of you both. Though, you must know, I always have been. I passed Dylan on my way to you. He's sound asleep. I took the liberty of placing some healing herbs on his wounds, which were not grave in any case."

Cam glanced at Alex. *Why does he sound that way?* she silently asked. *So serious* —

Alex had been wondering the same thing. "Are you going to leave us?" she blurted.

"I came to find Ileana," Karsh said, finessing the question. "Your guardian worked very hard during a recent trial, and it's affected her health. But not seriously."

The last phrase was clearly meant for Ileana. "In fact, with a little rest, perhaps some reading — I have several volumes that would be of interest to her. I think you'd particularly enjoy *Forgiveness or Vengeance:*

Righting Ancient Wrongs," he told the still-weeping witch. "She'll be fine, stronger than ever, in fact."

The warlock glanced quickly, suspiciously, over his shoulder.

Alex tried to pick up whatever it was Karsh had heard. By concentrating very hard, she could make out distant footsteps. They might belong to deer wandering as they grazed or rabbits scrambling through the under-brush, but they sounded as if they came from creatures that were bigger, clumsier.

Or, Cam got into it, taking off from Alex's thoughts, *some of those icky, touchy-feely spirits we passed on the way in.*

Suddenly, Ileana shuddered. She looked up at Karsh. "What have you done? I know this. I smell it," she said, alarmed.

"You see, my astute witch —" He paused, but Ileana did not demand that he call her goddess. "Your senses . . . your sensibilities . . . are already improving."

Ileana stood abruptly. "It's danger I smell. Not who or what brings it," she complained.

Taking their cue from Ileana, Alex sniffed the air, while Cam squinted to scan the outer edges of the circle.

"Ugh. Cheap cologne and oily hair tonic can so not cover up ripe body odor," Alex analyzed the fumes.

"Cheap cologne . . . Did you hear her?" Ileana's eyes

widened. She seized Karsh's lapels and searched his ruddy face. "It could only be . . . What are they doing here? How did they find us?"

Karsh shook his head. "I'm afraid it's my fault," he said sadly. "They must have followed me —"

"Who are they?" Alex asked, listening intently to the noises in the woods. Whoever was out there reeked memorably. And, though they were huffing and puffing rather than talking, their mean and manic thoughts sounded distantly familiar to her.

"I know them," Cam said all at once. "I mean, I've seen them before. Als, it's Dumb and Dumber, the dorks from the bowling alley —"

"Right!" That was exactly who they sounded like, the two weird strangers who'd dissed Cam's game a couple of weeks back. No one knew them or remembered seeing them before, but they were at the bowling alley that night — one stumpy, the other tall, both sourly checking out Alex and Cam.

Now, suddenly, they'd crashed through the trees and were standing in the moonlit clearing. Hunched over, their arms dangling apelike at their sides, their beady eyes were fixed on Ileana.

Who actually looked frightened.

Ileana, afraid? Impossible, Cam thought.

Alex had a similar take on Karsh. The ancient warlock was glaring at the intruders with withering scorn. She'd never seen the gentle tracker look so disgusted.

"What do you want?" he asked the boys, not bothering to disguise his disdain.

"Not you." Vey, the fireplug-shaped weight lifter, laughed. He trundled past Karsh, elbowing the old man out of his way, and went straight for Ileana.

Tsuris, his brother, slunk swiftly around Cam and Alex and approached the alarmed witch from the other side.

Do something! Alex silently urged Ileana. *Turn them into the worms they are; paralyze them with a gray-eyed glare; transport them to another universe.*

If Ileana heard her, she gave no sign.

"I am not responsible for sending your father to jail," she was trying to tell Vey. She spun around as Tsuris crept up behind her. "Your father, Fredo, confessed to a heinous crime," she told him. "He killed his brother. That's why he was put away."

They're Fredo's sons? Cam asked her sister.

Oh, please, no. Alex groaned. *That makes them . . . Our cousins!*

Suddenly, the brothers lunged at Ileana.

Karsh raised both his arms, his embroidered cape flaring wide behind him. A sparkling substance that resembled liquid confetti flew from his hands, falling like colored rain on Tsuris and Vey.

Tsuris, the taller of the oafs — his face now rainbow-streaked — fell to his knees. He grabbed at Ileana's blue robe as he went down, tearing its already bedraggled hem.

His brother, Vey, less speckled, shook his head, like a dog drying itself. Colored splotches flew from him.

A splash of scarlet landed on Alex's shoulder. The liquid seeped through her waterproof jacket and flannel shirt, leaving a pleasant puddle of heat on her skin — and the certainty that she could no longer move her shoulder.

It was a totally bizarre feeling. She knew she was not paralyzed, not technically, not physically, but she could not — would not — move, first her shoulder and then, as the sensation flowed downward, her arm and hand.

"Go!" she heard Karsh call to Ileana as Tsuris and Vey stumbled around the shaking blond witch. "Go home now. Rest. And *read,* my goddess! Read, as I instructed you. Go now. Run."

But Ileana was frozen to the spot. She stood staring down at the writhing Technicolor-splashed brothers.

"Come on," Cam cried to Alex. "There's something

wrong with her. Her mojo's gone south. And she can't move."

"I totally relate," Alex said, willing her hand to flex, her arm to raise. Well, her feet still worked, she remembered, and she dashed after Cam to the center of the circle where Ileana stood paralyzed by confetti or fright.

As she reached for Ileana, a hand circled Cam's ankle and held her fast. She looked down to see Tsuris hanging on to her. She tried to shake him off but his grip was iron tight.

"Get off me, you skanky goon!" she heard her sister cry.

When she looked up, Cam saw that Vey was standing behind Alex and had both his hammy arms around her neck. His snarling face was pressed against her ear. "It's not your turn," he sneered. "First we take care of cousin Ileana. Then maybe we'll figure out what to do with you —"

Alex barely heard him. All she wanted was his cologne-sprayed sweat, wet lips, and greasy hair as far from her as she could get them. She spun with all her might, lifting her knee at the same time.

With a deafening "HOOOF," Vey's arms spread, releasing her. And then they folded across his gut, and he keeled over. His large head splashed into a puddle of blue confetti.

"Hey!" Tsuris called to Alex, still clasping Cam's ankle. "You can't do that!"

"I am her guardian and I say, yes, she can!" Suddenly, Ileana stepped forward on her one good shoe, forward onto Tsuris's wrist. She ground her pointy heel into his leathery tanned skin — and his clenched fingers opened.

Cam quickly withdrew her foot. "You go, girl," she hollered. "And I mean, really. Go, Ileana. Do what Karsh said!"

Tsuris was holding his wrist and rocking back and forth. Alex rushed over to him and brushed the remains of the liquid red confetti from her jacket onto the howling man's back. His rocking and howling stopped at the same time. He tried to turn, to see who had done that to his back, then realized he couldn't move. His thin face froze in a glare of disbelief and betrayal.

"No," Ileana told Cam. "I can't. I won't." Looking over at Karsh, she said, "I can't. Please, please don't ask me to leave you now."

The old warlock went to her and gently took her arm. "Silly goddess. Let me walk you to the road —"

"Karsh, my friend, my mentor, my only father — please," Ileana begged. *Let me wait with the boy,* Alex heard her thinking. And Karsh did, too. *I'll stay with young Dylan. He'll be frightened if he wakes alone in the forest. Please, Karsh, don't send me away now.*

Alex looked at Cam. But her sister had heard only what their guardian witch had said aloud. Why, Alex wondered, would Ileana, who was always in a hurry, who always claimed she had "bigger fish to fry" and "places to go, people to see," whose very life was in danger here, be so reluctant to leave?

"Come." Karsh led Ileana through the aisle of tall trees toward the glen where Dylan slept.

"What are we supposed to do now?" Cam asked, looking warily at their out-of-commission cousins.

"Phone Dave and Emily?" Alex suggested, though she had no idea what to tell them other than that Dylan was safe. She supposed that was enough.

"How's your shoulder?" Cam asked.

Alex stretched. "Feels okay. That stuff didn't last all that long."

"Well, that's good," Cam said. They heard a noise behind them. "Or maybe not?" she whispered.

"Change of plans!" Vey lifted his head from the dirt; his little pig's eyes twinkled mischievously. Heaving himself up, he said, "Congratulations! You just moved to the head of the list!"

Tsuris was already sitting up. The sullen look on his face melted to one of glee as he got to his feet and focused on Alex.

"Um, we're witches," she said, backing up. "Just want to remind you."

He laughed and kept on coming.

"Yeah, girl witches," Alex heard Vey mock. "*Little girl witches —*"

"Actually, my sister's got some pretty *hot* tricks." Alex didn't dare take her eyes off Tsuris. She couldn't see Cam, but she was reasonably sure her twin had gotten the message. To make certain, she sent her a telepathic IM. *Fire up your eyes; let's fry these hot dogs —*

Too late, Cam's response came flying back.

Alarmed, Alex turned.

Vey had her sister pushed face-first against a tree. All Cam could burn in that direction was the trunk. The low-to-the-ground greaser was reaching for a rock. His pudgy fingers strained toward one that was big enough to do serious damage.

Alex took a step in Cam's direction. A burst of pain tore through her scalp as Tsuris held her back by her spiky hair.

"Where you going, little witchy?" he crooned cruelly. "Plenty of rocks around here. Enough for both of you. How do you think you'd look with your head all streaked red?"

Alex wriggled in Tsuris's grasp. "Been there, done

that," she said with more bravado than she felt. She thought about moving something — a rock, a branch, a fistful of dirt — tossing it at her captor telekinetically. But she couldn't focus on anything. He was moving her too fast, leading her by the hair to the tree where Cam was being held.

"Want to do it together?" he asked his brother. "Like it'll be one, two, and on three, we'll hit 'em in the head with stones, okay?"

Vey had finally managed to grab one of the rocks from the circle. "Okay, hurry," he said.

Still hanging on to Alex's hair, Tsuris crouched down to choose a stone of his own. He was really making a production of it. Painfully arched in a back bend, Alex could hear him mumbling, trying to decide on which one would best do the job — the job of smashing her head.

From that upside-down view she saw Karsh approaching. She didn't actually see him as much as deduce from the moonlit glitter and gold of what had to be his cape that he had returned to the clearing.

He saw the brutish louts lifting their stones. He was far enough away to be safe, Alex realized, feeling the strangest rush of relief.

Then suddenly, he was beside them, breaking Tsuris's and Vey's hold on the twins, spinning the brutes away with a strength no man his age could muster. "You will not harm them," Karsh declared.

Startled, Fredo's sons turned toward him together. The wizened warlock was standing between them and the stunned girls. Together, as mindlessly as they did everything, they hurled their rocks at him.

Alex shrieked as Karsh went down. Cam held the tree to keep her knees from buckling. They saw Karsh crumble. His magnificent golden cape fluttered about him, then settled over his face like a shroud.

CHAPTER NINETEEN
THE IMPOSSIBLE

Tsuris and Vey were examining the fallen warlock.

Cam didn't have to concentrate very hard at all. Every cell in her body seemed to be focused on the brothers with white-hot rage.

Alex had to slow her mind to choose just one torture for them. She settled on a broken branch a few feet behind them.

"Light it," she ordered Cam, not bothering to whisper or send her wish silently.

"I'm on it," her sister replied as the tip of the dry wood nearest Tsuris and Vey burst into flames.

It had never been easier for Alex to make something float, turn, and fly. The burning branch tumbled toward Fredo's sons.

Vey felt it first. "Hey!" he shouted, turning to see what had crashed into his back. What he saw, even before he felt it, was fire gnawing his too-tight T-shirt and hungrily attacking his trousers.

Tsuris was less lucky. The flying limb lit his scruffy bleached head. It must have made him feel, Alex thought with satisfaction, like she'd felt when the smarmy bully was leading her around by the hair.

This was the scene Ileana limped into a moment later. At first she saw only the hopping, flapping, flaming villains. But as they tore past her, heading for the bay, her tired gray eyes beheld Karsh's fallen body. Like a thermometer plunged into snow, the little color she had left drained from her.

Cam and Alex took her hands, as much for their own comfort as for hers. Ileana pushed them away. Without taking her eyes from Karsh, she removed her shoe and, barefoot, not noticing the sharp pebbles, pine needles, and twigs in her path, she walked slowly to him.

The ancient tracker was breathing with difficulty. His every gasp resounded through the forest, which slowly seemed to thicken again with the density of spirits.

Cam saw them. Her eyes wide with awe, she watched gauzy figures weave through the branches. They dipped and sailed, each passing low over Karsh, then swirling away, as if in pain, to form a circle within the circle.

Alex heard them. Moaning mournfully, keening, calling to one another. Among them she recognized the single voice she'd heard earlier. The one that had begged her not to lead him who loved her — him, who she now knew was Karsh — into danger. *Abigail Antayus,* another specter called the ghostly name, *he is of your clan.*

Ileana knelt beside Karsh. Her cold hands gently brushed the dirt from his brow, tenderly touched the almost-invisible indentation where one of the stones had found its mark.

"Goddess," Karsh wheezed, trying to smile.

"No," Ileana whispered. "Save your strength —"

"No need," he said, closing his eyes. "Dearest child. Listen."

Over the terrible screaming in her head, above Cam's inner voice and her own, both crying, *No, no, no,* Alex strained to hear Karsh's words.

"Why Thantos denied you is . . . more complex than you know," he rasped. "There is a curse, Ileana. And a hope. Your future and the twins' destiny is bound to it —"

Cam tugged at Alex's hand. "I want to hear him," she said. "Come with me. I want to be near him."

"Yes, come." Ileana beckoned them. "Come quickly."

They crossed to the center of the circle, where moonlight fell onto Karsh's once fearsome but now serene face. They knelt beside him, across from Ileana, waiting for him to speak again.

Clutching Cam's hand, Alex waited. Staring dry-eyed, empty, at his moonlit features, Ileana waited.

With his last breath, Karsh whispered, "Children, dearest ones, it is written. All is written."

CHAPTER TWENTY
THE RETURN

Ileana arrived at her own cottage at daybreak. Karsh's old friend Lady Rhianna had insisted that she get some rest.

Rhianna was an impressive witch in the best of times; she was positively fearsome and overwhelming now in the worst. She and the Exalted Elders of Coventry's Unity Council would see to Lord Karsh, the buxom witch decreed. To his corpse, Ileana reminded herself. Lord Karsh, friend Karsh, father and counselor, was dead.

Boris, Ileana's marmalade cat, waited on the doorstep. He looked bedraggled and forlorn as he rubbed against her torn blue hem. Everything looked forlorn, every creature on the island, as if the news of Karsh's passing had arrived before their procession had.

Such a sad parade it was. Ileana, silent, bereft, guided by the dark and solemn Rhianna — who had come at once, who'd known a moment after it happened that the beloved warlock was dead — and by Lord Grivveniss, another who had felt the empty wind of Karsh's passing. Six young and sturdy bearers, two witches and four warlocks whom he had counseled and tutored, carried the bier on which he lay — Karsh in his golden shroud.

The moment they'd touched foot on the island, the crowd began to assemble. Many had been waiting at the dock for their arrival. The procession passed through columns of mourners lining the path to the Council Dome. Which was where Lady Rhianna had issued her order to Ileana — to leave the Elders to their sad task and to go home and rest.

Now she found she dared not enter her own door. Her house had been ransacked by Karsh's murderers. Her hand on the latch alone was enough to set her stomach churning, roiling with hatred and a burning ache for revenge. Such emotions, Karsh had taught, would rob her of what strength and power she still owned.

Ileana turned away from her home. Accompanied by a mournfully yowling Boris, she walked barefoot along the well-worn path from her door to Karsh's cottage.

He was still there. His earth-sweet scent and robust spirit filled the little house. Ileana allowed herself to take it all in, with her burning eyes and gentle touch — his teapot on the stove, his form carved by time into the worn leather armchair beside the fireplace.

She felt the fragrant scratch of drying herbs hanging from ceiling beams, the cool marble of the counter on which sat potions and oils, seedlings and blossoming flowers, the myriad stones and candles he used to heal and help.

She ran her hand over the cluttered bookshelves, over the cracked spines of countless thick volumes, until a shocking vibration, an almost electric charge, shook her cold fingers as they passed over the flaking cover of *Forgiveness or Vengeance*.

The charge tingled through her entire being. She pulled the book from the shelf and carried it over to Karsh's chair. The moment she sat, exhaustion overtook her. Images, voices, feelings came with such force and speed that she thought, like Miranda, grief would drive her crazy.

Why she thought of Brice now was incomprehensible to her. With so much else to make her miserable, why should his handsome face, his eyes begging her forgiveness, come to mind? Because, now more than ever, she imagined Karsh's voice rasping, *You need love, my stubborn goddess. And this man, this warlock, loves you.*

No, Ileana told herself, told the imagined voice of Karsh, the one man she'd completely loved and trusted. Karsh. Now even he had abandoned her.

Appalled at her own selfishness, Ileana shook her head, trying to rid herself of such a shameful thought. She must be going mad. Miranda had. Miranda, the woman she'd so admired, in her youth the nearest thing Coventry had to a princess.

Where was Miranda? Ileana could not remember seeing her among the mourners this morning. Suddenly, she feared for the twins' mother. Already weak and unsettled, would the terrible news of Karsh's death throw Miranda back into madness?

As swiftly as Ileana's concern rose, it ebbed. She hadn't seen Thantos, either, she realized. Maybe they were together — "comforting" each other at Crailmore, the ugly gray castle overlooking the sea.

Thantos's fortress. Ileana's birthplace. The stone citadel where her mother, Beatrice, had died.

It's more complex than you know, Karsh had begun to explain to her.

Ileana closed her eyes now and let the memory of his words wash over her. *Why Thantos denied you*

is . . . more complex than you know. There is a curse . . . and a hope. Your future and the twins' destiny is bound to it —

The volume in her lap seemed too dense and heavy to open. She knew that inside it she would find the answer to Karsh's riddle. He had written it down. Knowing he was to die, he had spent his precious last days concerned with her welfare and that of the T'Witches.

And Karsh *had* known he would die. He had put on his funeral robes himself. The embroidered gold cloak. The medallion he'd worn when, years before Rhianna's appointment, he had headed the Unity Council. His beautiful bare features, timeworn, weathered, but carved with the same depth and integrity as his soul. He had known.

But would he have died had he not followed her? Was it the time or the place that had assured his death? If he'd stayed safely on Coventry . . .

Impossible.

Impossible that Karsh would have left the twins in the care of a powerless witch, even if she was their guardian. Impossible that he would not have rushed to their aid whether it meant his death or not. Such was his depth and integrity; such was his soul.

And who would guard them now? Their mother? She, who knew less of them than any disinterested schoolmate or salesgirl would know, whose knowledge was filtered through Thantos's self-serving tales, whose magick powers lay shattered in the ruins of her once-awesome mind?

Would Ileana, sworn to help and heal them, be up to the task? Weakened by all the things Karsh had tried, over and over, to caution her against — self-pity, rage, jealousy, resentment, the desire for vengeance . . .

How could she do her job now? How, without ridding herself of the very flaws that seemed to be her birthright — the ugly legacy of Thantos DuBaer, her father?

Too many questions, too few answers. Ileana's eyes closed. As she drifted off to sleep, her hands rested on the book, which contained her real inheritance — the truth, which Lord Karsh Antayus had bequeathed her.

CHAPTER TWENTY-ONE
GUARDIANS

The Marble Bay police delivered Dylan, Alex, and Cam home. To Dave and Emily, who'd been alerted immediately that their missing son had been found, the black-and-white squad car in the driveway was a prayer answered.

Not that Emily hadn't nearly passed out. Only the buoyant sound of Dave shouting, "He's okay! The girls, too! Em — they're all safe!" kept her from losing consciousness.

Emily flew to her son, smothering him with hugs and kisses, scolding him for running away, brushing back his hair to check the scratches on his face, and finally shuffling him inside the house — all through tears of joy and relief.

Dave hugged the twins, then hung back to talk to the police officers who had ferried the kids home. They informed him of the cell phone calls they'd gotten from Camryn and that they'd found his family right where his daughter said they'd be — on the shoulder of the road, near the woods outside of Salem.

Dylan's return led directly to a full confession-session — one that Cam and Alex neither wanted nor were asked to be part of. They heard bits and pieces of Dyl's download, enough to know that their brother was coming totally clean with his parents, delivering the good intent, the bad carry-through, the ugly ending.

"Your heart was in the right place, but your head was in the clouds. How could you think you could do this alone?" Dave struggled to keep the emotion out of his voice, but it was clear he was proud of his son. "Your mother and I admire you for trying to stop an evil, evil man, but —"

"You could have been killed!" Emily was still an emotional wreck and did little to hide it.

All the while, Dylan sat on the sofa between his parents. His head was in his hands, but the relief in the house was palpable. Cam and Alex felt it, too, especially because neither Dave nor Emily seemed to take much notice of them.

Which was just the way they wanted it.

Numbly, silently, Cam and Alex trudged upstairs, twin faces wearing one mask of sorrowful bewilderment. Their shock had yet to yield to full-out grief. Neither of them had the energy to talk or the will to think — let alone care very much about what was on the other's mind.

Cam went straight to the shower and turned it to HOT. She scrubbed so hard, red splotches broke out all over her fair skin. The smudges from the tree "Cousin" Vey had pushed her against came off easily, as did the mud from the woods. That was surface dirt. Ridiculous, irrational as it was, what Cam wanted most was to scrub away all that was underneath, all the events of the past year.

She wanted to go back. Press REWIND, then tape over the frightening drama her life had become. Just to be Emily and Dave's daughter again, Dylan's big sister, alpha girl among her friends, A+ student at her school, boy-magnet, and soccer star. That couldn't be too much to want; it was everything she'd had.

To retrieve that, Cam thought, she'd be more than willing to give the rest back: the stranger named Miranda, the fierce witch Ileana, even Alex if she had to. And him, too. The gentle soul who'd always understood when no one else seemed to. It was too hard to even think his name. To form a picture of Karsh was to fall apart. It would mean she'd have to confess what she now knew completely: Heartache was more than an overused song lyric. The pulsating muscle called the heart actually could ache. She could feel it.

Cam turned off the shower and stepped out onto the plush bath mat. As she shook the water out of her hair — forcefully, angrily, violently — she screamed silently, *No! No! No!*

No! This could *not* have happened. Not to Karsh. This could not *be* happening. Not to her.

Scaring herself suddenly, ridiculously, a manic laugh escaped her. Cam pressed the towel tightly against her mouth, her face, to muffle the sound.

Maybe this wasn't happening, she thought crazily. What if all of it — from the day she'd met Alex to now — turned out to be just some big, weird, beyond-bizarre dream?

What if, like a character on a TV soap, she'd wake to the reality that none of this had actually occurred, that maybe the rickety old Ferris wheel on which she'd thought she'd first seen a girl who was identical to her had really crashed, leaving Cam in a comatose state all this time?

AMAZING BUT TRUE, the tabloid headlines would read, COMA GIRL WAKES UP!

Wrapping herself in a soft, thick terry robe, Cam

slid to the floor, her back against the bathtub, head bowed, knees pressed to her face.

In the next room, in a nearly identical position, Alex had curled up on Cam's window seat. She'd swiped Miranda's quilt from the pile of clothes Cam had dumped on the floor and pulled it tight around her. It hugged her shoulders. Alex's scalp still hurt from Tsuris's cruel hair-pulling. Her eyes burned, too, from unshed tears.

She had tried to shut down, to feel nothing. She feared that if she let them, her emotions would come flooding in and surely drown her. In one short year, Alex had lost so much: her beloved Sara and — even though she despised him — the stepmonster, Ike.

And now Karsh.

Ileana, though alive, was a basket case; ditto, Miranda. They could not comfort her now.

Gone, too, was the life she used to know. A harder life, but a simpler one for sure.

Yet when Alex thought about going back, she knew she couldn't. She was different now. She had changed. She would never be as innocent, as naive, as dumb again.

And yet, how dumb had she actually been? She'd heard the voice calling out to her: *If you love him, go back. For the sake of him who loves you, go now. Do not lead him this way.*

She'd heard the words and hadn't known who they

were for or what they meant. Defying its warning had gotten Karsh killed.

Someone was coming up the steps. Alex was too wiped out to leap up and bolt the door. It didn't matter anyway. The person about to enter was someone she could probably deal with.

"Harry?" a soft voice called. Dylan poked his head into the room.

"Hey, Dudley," Alex answered flatly.

They were stupid names they'd made up for each other. Dylan had jokingly dubbed Alex "Harry Potter," since she was an orphan coming to live with them; Alex had retorted that that had to make him wicked cousin Dudley. Only between themselves had those "sicknames," as they called them, stuck.

Dylan went straight for the window seat, forcing Alex to squeeze over. She threw her arm around the boy, who rested his head on her shoulder.

For a while, neither spoke.

Then Dylan said, "It just seemed —"

"Like a good idea at the time?" On automatic, Alex finished the cliché. Staring out the window, she said, "You gotta know, Dudley, that was a stupido stunt of epic proportions."

"I know," he said. "I should never have gone alone —"

"Ya think?" Alex said sarcastically.

"I'm an idiot, right?" the contrite boy offered.

"Yeah, but you're our idiot. The Barneses' village idiot." Alex tousled Dylan's hair. "It takes a village to raise an idiot."

Dylan shrugged. "I'm grounded."

Alex pretended to be shocked. "Whoa, that's harsh, bro. But you know what? I hear the warden clomping up the steps. You'd best be gone."

Alex wasn't kidding. Dylan dove for the bathroom that connected their rooms — startling Cam — and just missed his father by a nanosecond.

"Can I come in?" Dave asked gently.

"*Mi casa es su casa*," Alex said.

"You all right?" Dave searched her face for signs of bruising.

"I'll . . ." She almost said, "live," but choked on it. Alex quickly averted her eyes so Dave wouldn't suspect she was about to lose it.

"Cam in there?" he asked, nodding toward the open door of the bathroom.

"Daddy . . ." Still wrapped in her robe, Cam suddenly ran over and pressed her face against his shirtfront. Dave wrapped bearlike arms around his daughter and patted her back as he used to when she was little. That's when Cam broke down.

"He's dead, Daddy," she wailed. "Karsh is . . . he . . . got killed." She pulled away and looked into her dad's eyes. "Karsh, who gave me to you —"

Dave swallowed hard. He'd realized the girls were upset, emotional — but after what the cops and Dylan had just told him, he figured it was all about their daring rescue. He'd come upstairs, in fact, to tell the girls that thanks to Cam's 911, the perv had been picked up and would soon be behind bars for a long time. He'd come to congratulate them. It hadn't occurred to him he'd be comforting them. Feeling his own grief about the strange but kindly man who'd entrusted the baby Cam to him would have to come later.

Now he patted Cam's back and gently said, "Oh, baby, this is your first brush with death. I'm so sorry." He reached out to include Alex in his embrace. To his surprise, she actually allowed him to put an arm around her shoulder.

It wasn't until later, after all the phone calls — from Dave's and Emily's friends, from Cam's and Alex's pals, from the newspaper wanting an interview with Dylan (which Dave nixed) — that Cam and Alex were finally ready to talk.

"It's our fault, Cam." Alex fell onto her bed, where Miranda's quilt still lay. Her voice full of remorse, she tried to explain what she'd heard the spirits tell her. She said she should have told Cam, told someone. . . . Maybe then, Karsh wouldn't be dead.

Cam was so not buying it. It wasn't about dodging blame, she insisted as she paced the room, shaking her head. "Als? I don't know much about what's happened, or why. But in my bones I know this. We didn't kill Karsh. It was his time. He knew it; Ileana knew it. We'd have known it, too, if we'd grown up on Coventry; we'd have recognized the burial robe. But we heard what he was saying and the way he was talking.

"Karsh was our tracker, the man who kept us from going crazy when we were kids. He was a wise, brilliant, kindly human being who just happened to be a powerful warlock. The Karsh we knew would have chosen to go out this way, shielding Ileana, protecting us."

Alex's tears fell on Miranda's quilt.

Cam planted herself on her bed, drew her knees to her chest, and rocked back and forth. For a while, she was quiet. Then she whispered, "Alex? I'm freaked. Thantos — and now those hideously creepy cousins — they're so not done with us. Please don't think I'm selfish, but I'm really scared. Who's going to protect us? Who'll be our guardian?"

With a defiant swipe, Alex blotted her eyes on the quilt. She inhaled its sweet fragrances and lifted her chin. "I will."

"Will what?" Cam stared at her twin.

"I'll be your guardian, your protector — and you'll be mine," Alex declared.

"Can we do that? Protect ourselves?" Cam wrinkled her forehead.

"The other choice would be?" Alex began to feel stronger, surer of herself. She leaped off her bed and jumped so hard onto Cam's that her sister bounced.

"Here's the sitch, Sista T'Witch," Alex teased. "In this corner, we've got one glitzy but grieving guardian-goddess. In the other? A messed-up mom. Baddies of all ages and abilities — plenty we probably haven't even had the pleasure of meeting yet — are after us. And remember," she said more seriously now, "what Karsh said, about there being a curse."

"A curse and a hope," Cam remembered. "Ileana's destiny and ours are tied to it."

"Like it or not, want it or not." Alex tilted her head toward Cam. "It's up to us now."

Cam tilted hers so that it touched Alex's. "And we are so up for it. All of it."

ABOUT THE AUTHORS

H.B. Gilmour is the author of numerous best-selling books for adults and young readers, including the *Clueless* movie novelization and series; *Pretty in Pink,* a University of Iowa Best Book for Young Readers; and *Godzilla,* a Nickelodeon Kids Choice nominee. She also cowrote the award-winning screenplay *Tag*.

H.B. lives in upstate New York with her husband, John Johann, and their misunderstood dog, Fred, one of the family's five pit bulls, three cats, two snakes (a boa constrictor and a python), and five extremely bright, animal-loving children.

Randi Reisfeld has written many best-sellers, such as the *Clueless* series (which she wrote with H.B.); the *Moesha* series; and biographies of Prince William, New Kids on the Block, and Hanson. Her Scholastic paperback *Got Issues Much?* was named an ALA Best Book for Reluctant Readers in 1999.

Randi has always been fascinated with the randomness of life . . . About how any of our lives can simply "turn on a dime" and instantly (*snap!*) be forever changed. About the power each one of us has deep inside, if only we knew how to access it. About how any of us would react if, out of the blue, we came face-to-face with our exact double.

From those random fascinations, T'Witches was born.

Oh, and BTW: She has no twin (that she knows of) but an extremely cool family and cadre of BFFs to whom she is totally devoted.